Making Waves

For my parents, who have always valued a nurtured imagination.

Making Waves
Three Radio Plays

Emil Sher

SIMON & PIERRE
A MEMBER OF THE DUNDURN GROUP
TORONTO · OXFORD

Simon & Pierre
A Member of the Dundurn Group

Editor: Marc Côté
Design: Scott Reid
Printer: Transcontinental Printing Inc.

Sher, Emil, 1959-
    Making waves: three radio plays

Contents: Mourning dove — Denial is a river — Past imperfect.
ISBN 0-88924-283-6

I. Title
PS8587.H3853M34 1998   C812'.54   C98-931576-2
PR9199.3.S5118M34 1998

1 2 3 4 5   02 01 00 99 98

We acknowledge the support of the **Canada Council for the Arts** for our publishing program. We also acknowledge the support of the **Ontario Arts Council** and the **Book Publishing Industry Development Program** of the **Department of Canadian Heritage.**

THE CANADA COUNCIL | LE CONSEIL DES ARTS
FOR THE ARTS | DU CANADA
SINCE 1957 | DEPUIS 1957

Simon & Pierre
8 Market Street
Suite 200
Toronto, Ontario, Canada
M5E 1M6

Simon & Pierre
73 Lime Walk
Headington, Oxford
England
OX3 7AD

Simon & Pierre
2250 Military Road
Tonawanda, NY
U.S.A. 14150

Contents

ACKNOWLEDGEMENTS

The magic of a radio play — distilled voices ignited in a listener's mind — is more than mere sleight of hand. All is not what meets the ear. Several people contribute to creating a show, directly and otherwise.

As a producer, Gregory J. Sinclair brought the perfect touch to *Mourning Dove* and *Denial is a River*, both generously commissioned by Willy Barth when he was senior producer at *Morningside*. Producer James Roy brought a seasoned, insightful eye to *Past Imperfect*, knowing when to stoke a play, and when to let it breathe. As a story editor, Dave Carley asked all the right questions. I am grateful to all the associate producers — Kate Nickerson, Nina Callaghan, Sandra Broitman, Colleen Woods — whose task is so important, and so easy to take for granted. Casting director Linda Grearson has a knack for arranging well-suited marriages between a role and an actor's voice. Ann Jansen and Heather Brown offered a continuous flow of support in untold hallway conversations at the CBC. Josie Phelan is nothing less than an administrative angel. As head of Radio Performance, Damiano Pietropaolo's commitment to radio drama in the face of cutbacks inspires those of us who continue to have faith in the form. Special thanks to Barbara Brown and David Wyman for their help when this book was still a manuscript.

My wife Kathy's unconditional support has been a daily balm. My young daughters Sophie and Molly remind me that make believe is what you make of it.

Mourning Dove

Mourning Dove was first broadcast on *Morningside* on January 30, 1996 with the following cast:

DOUG RAMSAY	R.H. Thomson
SANDRA RAMSAY	Martha Burns
TINA RAMSAY	Annick Obonsawin
KEITH MARTEL	David McFarlane
CORPORAL CRAIG PIERCE	Ken James
GORDON BELLAIR	Robert Parson
BARCLAY	Jonathan Welsh
CHISHOLM	Philip Akin
DR. KOVACS	Maggie Huculak
JUDGE	Lynne Deragon
ELDON	Wayne Ward
GWEN	Catherine Hayos
VERA	Kathryn Miller
ALBERT	Ross Manson

Producer	Gregory J. Sinclair
Production Assistant	Kate Nickerson
Recording Engineer	Janice Bayer
Sound Effects	Anton Szabo
Casting Director	Linda Grearson
Script Editor	Dave Carley

Please note that all the courtroom scenes and testimony are from the transcripts of an actual trial, with some modifications.

Scene One: Outside Tina's Bedroom

[*Sound: Tina's laboured breathing. Continues under:*]

SANDRA   *(Off)* Doug. *(Beat)* Doug. *(Approaching)* Come to bed.

[*Sound: Tina's breathing rises, then fades.*]

SANDRA   This has become a regular habit, you know, you standing there, watching her like some faithful dog. *(Pause)* I can't remember the last time you came straight to bed.

[*Sound: Doug coughs.*]

SANDRA   Every night, the same detour. *(Pause)* Standing there isn't going to change a thing. *(Pause)* I'm going to bed. You coming?

[*Sound: Faint breathing. Doug and Tina*]

SANDRA   Good night. *(Off)* Good night.

[*Sound: (Off) Sandra closes bedroom door. Sound: Tina moans. Doug exhales.*]

Scene Two (a): Courthouse Steps

[*Sound/biz: Media frenzy as reporters swarm around Doug Ramsay, shoving and shouting. Continues under:*]

REPORTER 1   Mr. Ramsay, how will you plead?

REPORTER 2   Did you talk it over with your wife?

REPORTER 3   Was it a question of mercy?

[*Sound: "Mercy" reverberates in a rapid succession of different inflections: a statement, a plea, a*] *question, a sneer, and finally, a whisper.]*

Scene Two (b): Courtroom

COURT CLERK Douglas J. Ramsay, would you stand up please. Indictment: Douglas J. Ramsay (born 7th of June 1953) in the Province of Alberta stands charged that on or about the 21st day of November, A.D. 1994 in the Province of Alberta he did unlawfully cause the death of Tina Catherine Ramsay and thereby commit first degree murder –

KEITH *(Off)* No. He didn't do it. Not Dougie. No, no.

[*Sound/biz:Mumbling and rumbling as court spectators react to outburst.*]

KEITH Not Tina. Never, never.

JUDGE Sit down or you will be escorted out of this courtroom. *(Beat)* Continue.

CLERK ...he did unlawfully cause the death of Tina Catherine Ramsay and thereby commit first degree murder contrary to Section 235 (1) of the <u>Criminal Code</u>. Douglas J. Ramsay, do you understand this charge that has been read to you, sir?

DOUGLAS Yes.

CLERK How do you plead?

DOUGLAS Not guilty.

Scene Three (a): Doctor's examination room (flashback)

[*Sound:Tina crying out in pain as she lies on table. Continues under:*]

SANDRA Okay, Tina, that's a girl. Dr. Kovacs is almost done. Almost.

DR. KOVACS Her left hip has a nice range. The right hip concerns me.

DOUGLAS She never lies down on her right side.

DR. KOVACS You can see how the skin on the left side is starting to break down.

SANDRA She favours that side. You know. It's more comfortable.

DR. KOVACS I want to try and move her right hip. I'll need your help.

SANDRA Daddy and I are going to turn you over, sweetheart. Okay?

DR. KOVACS On the count of three. One. Two. Three.

[*Sound/biz: Tina cries in pain as her body is shifted. Sandra whispers words of comfort.*]

DR. KOVACS Her right hip has no range. It's too –

DOUGLAS It's too painful.

[*Sound: A sharp cry from Tina.*]

DR. KOVACS *(Beat)* Yes.

Scene Three (b): Doctor's office

[*Sound: (off) a baby crying in waiting room.*
Sound: (off) phone ringing.]

RECEPTIONIST *(Off, into phone)* Dr. Kovacs' office.

[*Sound: Door closing, muffles waiting room sounds.*]

DR. KOVACS   Tina is going to need another operation.

                    [*A discomforting silence as the news sinks in. We
                    can hear – faintly – the infant crying in the
                    waiting room.*]

SANDRA   I remember what you did to her back. All those
                    rods and wires. I don't want you drilling any
                    more holes in my baby.

DR. KOVACS   I understand that, Mrs. Ramsay. But you've seen
                    what Tina's hip is doing to her. The pain it's
                    causing.

DOUGLAS   What about drugs? You know. Instead.

DR. KOVACS   I don't think so. We would have to use fairly
                    powerful drugs. If they're taken with the
                    medication she's using to control her seizures
                    there could be some serious side effects. It could
                    be even harder for her to swallow. Food could
                    end up in her lungs. She could get very sick.

SANDRA   No more. *(Beat)* No more.

DR. KOVACS   Tina's in too much pain to do nothing. Her hip
                    is too far gone.

DOUGLAS   What does that mean? Too far gone.

DR. KOVACS   We have to do what we call a salvage procedure.

SANDRA   Salvage?

DR. KOVACS   Try and picture the ball at the top of Tina's thigh
                    bone, and the hip socket it fits into. There's
                    something called "articular cartilage", a tissue
                    which allows this ball and socket to move freely.
                    The trouble is, Tina's ball has been sitting out of
                    its socket for too long. The ball is damaged and
                    has lost its shape. The cartilage has worn away.
                    We can't put the ball back into the socket.

SANDRA   Why not?

DR. KOVACS   It would be like putting an arthritic hip back together again. It's doomed to continue to be painful.

DOUGLAS   How are you going to do this salvage business?

DR. KOVACS   In simple terms, I have to take away the damaged part and cover the end of the bone with muscles, and hope –

DOUGLAS   What do you mean, "take away"?

DR.KOVACS   Remove.

DOUGLAS   You saw it off, don't you? You're gonna saw off the ball part.

DR. KOVACS   *(Pause)* The ball part and about the top quarter of the thigh bone.

                [*Sound: Sandra reacts.*]

DR. KOVACS   The surgery is necessary. We have no alternative.

DOUGLAS   That's not the end of it, is it? Half the kids with palsy they don't make it to their tenth birthday. You told us that. You showed us that study.

DR. KOVACS   Fifty percent survived past age ten. Tina is twelve.

DOUGLAS   No more operations?

DR. KOVACS   The chances of Tina's other hip dislocating is a real possibility. And because of her weight loss, I expect there may have to be more intervention.

DOUGLAS   Intervention.

DR. KOVACS   A feeding tube...

13

[*Sound: A bereft Sandra reacts.*]

DR. KOVACS   Or another method of giving her nutrition that would bypass the mouth and swallowing mechanism. But let's not jump too far ahead. We have to schedule Tina's hip surgery. The sooner, the better. I have an opening in three weeks. Let's do it then.

Scene Four (a): Ramsays' home - hallway (flashback)

[*Sound: Tina's laboured breathing. Continues under:*]

SANDRA   (*Off*) Doug. (*Approaching*) Doug. Come to bed. (*Pause*) We've got to get up early tomorrow. I don't want to be late for church. (*Beat*) You look tired. You look terrible. You shouldn't have gone into the store today. Not after what the doctor told us yesterday. You should've taken the day off. You should get some sleep.

[*Sound: Tina's breathing.*]

SANDRA   I'm going to bed. Good night. (*Off*) Good night.

[*Sound: Tina's breathing continues, cross-fades with a ticking clock in Ramsays' bedroom, which continues under:*]

Scene Four (b): Ramsays' home - bedroom

[*Sound/biz: Doug climbing into bed, Sandra being roused.*]

SANDRA   (*Groggy*) I didn't think you were ever coming to bed. What time is it?

DOUGLAS   What's the colour of pain?

SANDRA   What?

DOUGLAS   Pain. You think it has a colour?

SANDRA   *(Fully awake)* What are you talking about?

DOUGLAS   Today, at the store. Keith comes up to me, he's all upset. A customer had come up to him and said he needed some paint for his pane. What colour would Keith suggest?

SANDRA   A window pane.

DOUGLAS   You know how Keith can scramble words. Like when he carved Tina the mourning dove.

KEITH   *(Reverb)* To wake her up in the morning.

SANDRA   What'd you tell him about the colour of pain?

DOUGLAS   I told him what the customer meant. But I've been thinking about it ever since. If Tina's pain had a colour, what colour do you think it would be?

SANDRA   Red pain. Blue pain. What does it matter? Pain is pain.

DOUGLAS   A colour might make things easier.

SANDRA   For who?

                [*An uncomfortable pause.*]

SANDRA   I don't think Tina can take much more.

                [*Another pause.*]

DOUGLAS   Today I picked up a 40-pound bag of gravel. You know what went through my mind? This bag of gravel weighs more than my daughter.

15

SANDRA	Some nights, I wish she would just go to sleep and not wake up. *(An unearthly silence as both Sandra and Doug absorb Sandra's statement.)*

Scene Five: Ramsays' home: kitchen (flashback)

[*Sound:Bacon frying, kitchen sounds.*]

SANDRA	You going to church dressed like that?
DOUGLAS	I'm going into work.
SANDRA	Can't it wait?
DOUGLAS	I asked Gwen to look after Tina 'til I got back.
SANDRA	I thought we should both be there. Make our prayers twice as loud.
DOUGLAS	I'll take a raincheck.
SANDRA	Why're you opening up on a Sunday anyhow?
DOUGLAS	I didn't say I was opening up. I have work to do.
SANDRA	Even God rested on the seventh day.
DOUGLAS	God didn't own a hardware store.
SANDRA	I thought if we both went. I don't know. Maybe things would turn out all right.
DOUGLAS	I've said my prayers.
SANDRA	You want me to pick you up at the store, then? On the way back from church?
DOUGLAS	I'll meet you back here.

Scene Six (a): Ramsay's hardware store - back room (flashback)

[*Sound: Electric sander. The sander becomes louder as Doug approaches and enters back room of hardware store.*]

DOUGLAS   (*Over sound of sander*) Keith. (*Beat*) Keith.

[*Keith shuts off sander.*]

KEITH   I didn't hear you come in.

DOUGLAS   How could you, with that thing going a mile a minute. What are you doing here on a Sunday morning? Store's closed. You should be home.

KEITH   I want to finish this. For Tina. My sander wasn't working. I let myself in. Is that okay?

DOUGLAS   I wasn't expecting you.

KEITH   It's a birdhouse. See?

DOUGLAS   How long do you plan on being here?

KEITH   I have to finish sanding the roof.

DOUGLAS   I got some work to do.

KEITH   You think she'll like it?

DOUGLAS   I'm sure she will.

KEITH   You'll have to put in near her window. So she can look out and watch the birds.

DOUGLAS   I'll be out front if you need me.

KEITH   You think they'll like it?

DOUGLAS   What?

KEITH	The birds. You think they'll like the house?
DOUGLAS	For sure. *(Beat)* I have to get some work done.
KEITH	For sure.

[*Sound: Keith turns on sander. Fades.*]

Scene Six (b): Ramsay's hardware store *(flashback)*

KEITH	Is it okay if –
DOUGLAS	Christ, you scared me.
KEITH	I didn't want to bother you. You looked real busy. Like you were talking to someone who wasn't there.
DOUGLAS	How long have you been standing there?
KEITH	Couple of minutes.

(Uncomfortable silence.)

KEITH	Is it okay if I take a couple of sheets of sandpaper?
DOUGLAS	Help yourself to whatever you need.
KEITH	What's the hose for?
DOUGLAS	What do you mean, what's it for?
KEITH	I was just asking.
DOUGLAS	What does someone use a hose for?
KEITH	For watering.
DOUGLAS	Well, that's what it's for. It's for watering.

Scene Seven: Ramsays' home (flashback)

CHISHOLM   *(Reverb/courtroom)* Most importantly, you will also hear evidence on how Douglas Ramsay, on November 21st, once Sandra had gone to church with the kids, set about going to his hardware store, getting some pieces in terms of fittings and pipes together, getting some rags, putting them in the truck, then driving back home...

[*Sound: Hockey game play-by-play on the television.*
Sound: Doug closes door behind him as he walks into house..]

DOUGLAS   Gwen?

[*Sound: The game gets louder as Doug approaches living room.*]

DOUGLAS   A hockey game at this hour?

GWEN   Last night's game. I taped it.

DOUGLAS   What's the point of watching when you already know the score?

GWEN   I don't know. I kinda like knowing how things'll turn out before they begin.

DOUGLAS   Tina enjoying?

GWEN   I don't know. Not like before. She. She doesn't react like she used to.

DOUGLAS   Maybe the game's getting too fast for her.

GWEN   Maybe. *(Beat)* You want me to stay and help prepare lunch?

DOUGLAS   We're all right.

GWEN   You sure? I don't mind.

DOUGLAS   I'm sure.

GWEN   Okay, then.

            [*Sound: Gwen puts on coat.*]

GWEN   Bye, Tina. Bye, Mr. Ramsay.

            [*Sound: Gwen walks away. The game continues.*]

GWEN   Mr. Ramsay?

            [*Sound: More hockey noise. Doug is lost in thought.*]

GWEN   Mr. Ramsay?

            (*Douglas still doesn't react.*)

GWEN   (*More forcefully*) Mr. Ramsay.

DOUGLAS   (*Startled*) I. I didn't.

GWEN   I forgot my tape.

DOUGLAS   (*Lost*) The tape.

            [*Sound: The hockey crowd is silenced when tv is clicked off; video tape is ejected from vcr.*]

GWEN   Bye.

            [*Sound: Front door is closed.*]

DOUGLAS   Tina, sweetheart. It's time to go.

            [*Sound/biz: Doug picks up Tina and carries her in his arms.*]

CHISHOLM   (*Reverb/courtroom*) ...driving with Tina in the

20

truck out to the shed where she was then
propped up with the rags while he rigged an
apparatus up to run from the exhaust and
through the sliding window of the cab and
started the vehicle and then eventually shut the
vehicle off and returned Tina to her bed in the
house and there awaited the return of Sandra
and the children.

Scene Eight: Courtroom

PIERCE

I told him I wanted him to listen very carefully
because this was a serious matter. I started by
saying that we are not here to judge him. I
understand the situation you are in and we
empathize with you. We have no choice but to
do the job we have to but at the same time we'll
assist him in getting through this situation as
best we can. "We have spoken to several people.
Everyone said the same thing that you are a
caring person, a good person. At the same time,
we know that this was not a natural death. Your
daughter was in a great deal of pain. Doug,
after considering all that is known, I have no
doubt that you caused your daughter's death."
There was no response from him and I noticed
that his eyes were glassy with tears. I continued,
"This is not something that you wanted or
planned to do. You loved your daughter very
much." At that point he nodded yes. "This is
something that you felt you had to do out of
love for your daughter, isn't it, Doug?" There
was no reply. "I can imagine this is very difficult
for you and I feel bad." I repeated that he was a
loving father and I said,"You only did what you
felt was best for her out of love for your
daughter." Again there was no reply and I
repeated it. I asked, "Isn't that right, Doug?" At
that point he was close to crying. I said again,
"That's what happened, isn't it, Doug? Isn't that
right?" He replied, "My priority was to put her

21

out of her pain." I asked, "That's what you thought was right, wasn't it?" and he began nodding his head yes. At this point there were tears flowing freely.

Scene Nine: Ramsays' front steps (flashback)

[*Sound:(off) car engine is turned off; car door slammed shut.*]

DOUGLAS   How was church?

SANDRA   *(Approaching)* We'll have to wait and see.

DOUGLAS   What does that mean?

SANDRA   Why aren't you wearing your jacket?

DOUGLAS   Didn't notice.

SANDRA   You step out and figure it was still summer?

DOUGLAS   Didn't give it much thought.

SANDRA   Where's Tina?

DOUGLAS   Sleeping.

SANDRA   At this time of day?

DOUGLAS   What time is it?

SANDRA   One-thirty. When did she fall asleep?

DOUGLAS   About an hour ago.

SANDRA   She okay?

DOUGLAS   What do you mean?

SANDRA   How was she when she fell asleep?

DOUGLAS   *(Pause)* Peaceful.

SANDRA   Well, I hate to disturb the peace, but I gotta wake her up.

DOUGLAS   Now?

SANDRA   She's gotta eat.

DOUGLAS   I'm not hungry.

SANDRA   Are you okay?

Scene Ten: Courtroom

PIERCE   I asked him if he wanted to tell me how he did it. He says he drove the truck to the shed with her in it, hooked up a hose to the exhaust and ran it into the cab. I asked, "How long was she in there for?" and he replied but I don't recall what he said for a time and I asked, "And she just fell asleep?" He said, "Yes, she just fell asleep," and then he added, "If she'd have started to cry I would have taken her out of there," and then again he himself began to cry. *(Pause)* I said, "Doug, you have told us briefly what happened. I would like you to start at the very beginning and go through exactly what took place. Go slow. I'll put it to paper." He started, "She's been in pain for years. Ever since she was born she's had trouble." He hesitated. I said, "Go on." *(Pierce's voice cross-fades with Doug Ramsay's)* "She had an operation a year ago in August to straighten her back, put rods in."

DOUGLAS   Prior to that her hip was dislocated intermittently so they operated on her back. They knew there would be one on her hip but the hip was secondary, didn't seem that serious. Then since May or June almost full time dislocated. Each time you moved her there was pain so the

23

operation for the hip was planned for this time of year. It was more complicated than what we had expected so we just couldn't see another operation. She'd be confined to a cast for I don't know what the time was so I felt the best thing for her was that she be put out of her pain.

Scene Eleven: Ramsays' house (flashback)

[*Sound: Anxious knocking on front door. There is no reply. Anxious knocking resumes. More silence, until...*]

DOUGLAS   *(From behind door)* Who is it?

KEITH   Me.

[*Sound: Doug opens door.*
Sound:(off) Sandra's muffled, animal-like crying. Continues under:]

KEITH   I just finished it. What do you think?

DOUGLAS   Very nice.

KEITH   I painted the roof red. They like bright colours.

DOUGLAS   Maybe.

[*Sound: Sandra's crying intensifies, can be heard more clearly.*]

KEITH   Is that Tina?

DOUGLAS   *(Pause)* No.

KEITH   Can I show it to her?

DOUGLAS   *(Lost in thought)* What?

KEITH   The birdhouse. Can I show it to Tina?

DOUGLAS   When?

KEITH   I'll show it to her. Then we can put it up near
              her window.

DOUGLAS   No.

KEITH   You don't like it?

DOUGLAS   Not now.

KEITH   I can make another one.

DOUGLAS   Now is not a good time.

KEITH   When's a good time?

DOUGLAS   Leave it here for now.

KEITH   Tina won't see it down there.

DOUGLAS   Leave it here. *(Beat)* Please.

Scene Twelve: Coffee shop

[*Sound/biz: Clatter of cutlery, small talk in booths.
Gordon Bellair approaches Cpl. Pierce's booth, sets
down his coffee.*]

GORDON   Craig, you gotta minute?

PIERCE   You know what the service is like around here,
              Gordon. I got at least fifteen. What's on your
              mind?

GORDON   Keith.

PIERCE   Keith made a nuisance of himself in court
              today.

GORDON   I heard.

PIERCE	He didn't want to hear what I had to say about Doug. About what Doug had told me he'd done. He kept crying out, saying it wasn't true. The judge warned him twice, then threw him out of the courtroom.
GORDON	I know. He dropped by my place this afternoon.
PIERCE	That's not front-page news, Gordon. He spends half his life at your lumberyard, the other half at Doug's store.
GORDON	He didn't stick around. Usually he sticks around. You know. Collecting scraps of wood and whatnot. Today he was all funny like. Real nervous. Just stood around with his hands in his pockets. Then kinda disappeared.
PIERCE	Is there a moral to this story?
GORDON	I drove by Keith's apartment. To make sure he was alright. Mrs. Sanderson, she told me he never showed up for supper.
PIERCE	Keith's not one to miss a meal.
GORDON	He could be in danger. He could be. He doesn't. You know what Keith is like.
PIERCE	I don't have a crystal ball.
GORDON	My rifle's gone, too. The one I keep in the office.
PIERCE	Rifle?

[*The higher stakes suddenly spark Pierce's interest.*]

GORDON	I'm worried.
PIERCE	I'll look into it.

GORDON   I was wondering.

PIERCE   What were you wondering, Gordon?

GORDON   I was thinking maybe there was. I don't know. Some kind of connection.

PIERCE   What kind of connection?

GORDON   He was awfully attached to the girl. Always making her gifts out of wood. Maybe what happened to Tina set him off. Scared him. *(Beat)* You know. They were both. *(Pause)*

PIERCE   Both?

GORDON   *(A considered pause)* They were both different.

Scene Thirteen (a): Courtroom

JUDGE   Good morning. It is your job to decide the facts from the evidence you have heard, then to apply the law to those facts, and, having done that, to try and reach a verdict as to the guilt or otherwise of Douglas Ramsay. You cannot let your passions or your feelings stand in the way of your reason. The questions you must ask here are whether you are satisfied beyond a reasonable doubt that Douglas Ramsay did in fact cause the death of his daughter and, if so, did he do so intentionally. It is convenient here to deal with Mr. Barclay's argument. He says Tina's death should be characterized as a suicide, that all her life her parents were required to make her choices for her, and that they had a moral and legal obligation to make the proper choices – choices that were in her best interest, that she was entitled to commit suicide and that her legal guardians were authorized to make that choice for her because she was incapable of making it herself. I must tell you as a matter of

27

law that this argument is untenable. Mr. Chisholm says that this was a calculated, cold-blooded murder motivated by self-interest. The evidence did not leave that image in my mind and I doubt that most people would see it that way. Mr. Barclay says that if Mr. Ramsay did intentionally cause the death of his daughter by some means of unlawful act, then it was a compassionate act of kindness. That seems to be more likely. Each of you will have your own view but both characterizations beg the question which is, did Tina's father intentionally cause her death by means of some unlawful act, namely by putting her in the cab of the truck and polluting it with exhaust, and if so, was it planned and deliberate? First degree murder is one that is planned and deliberate. Murder that is not first degree is second degree murder. There are only three possible verdicts here guilty as charged, not guilty as charged but guilty of second degree murder, or not guilty.

Scene Thirteen (b): Courthouse steps

[*Sound/biz: A refrain of the melee that greeted Doug on the first day of the trial: a media frenzy as reporters swarm around Doug Ramsay, shoving and shouting.*]

REPORTER 1   How do you feel?

REPORTER 2   Did you want to speak in your own defense?

REPORTER 3   Do you think the jury believes you're innocent?

[*Sound: "innocent" reverberates in a rapid succession of different inflections: a statement, a plea, a question, a sneer, and finally, a whisper.*]

Scene Fourteen: Holding cell

[*Sound: The clank-and-grind of a metal jail door being closed and locked.*]

SANDRA   What d'you think's going to happen?

DOUGLAS   Don't know.

SANDRA   You might end up going to jail.

DOUGLAS   I might.

SANDRA   For a long time.

DOUGLAS   I know.

SANDRA   Jail is for criminals. You're not a criminal.

DOUGLAS   No.

SANDRA   Are you scared?

DOUGLAS   *(Pause)* No.

SANDRA   I am.

DOUGLAS   I'll be all right.

SANDRA   You know how sometimes you wish for something. Then it happens. Then you wonder if it would've happened if you hadn't wished so hard.

DOUGLAS   You don't think I should've done it.

SANDRA   I didn't say that.

DOUGLAS   What're you saying?

SANDRA   I feel guilty.

DOUGLAS   I'm the one on trial.

SANDRA   We've been through this together.

DOUGLAS   Always.

SANDRA   From the start. You and me.

DOUGLAS   And her.

SANDRA   And her.

DOUGLAS   I miss her.

SANDRA   It's been hard.

DOUGLAS   What would you have done?

SANDRA   I don't know.

DOUGLAS   What was I supposed to do?

SANDRA   You did what was best for her.

DOUGLAS   *(Pause)* That's right.

SANDRA   No one understands.

DOUGLAS   No. They don't. *(Beat)* Sometimes I don't.

SANDRA   They don't know what it's like.

DOUGLAS   I don't understand. Not always. Sometimes I
            don' t understand any of this. *(Beat)* Do you?

SANDRA   Not always. Not yet.

DOUGLAS   Green.

SANDRA   Green?

DOUGLAS   The colour of pain.

SANDRA   They found him, you know. Keith. Sitting on
          top of the fire tower. He won't budge.

DOUGLAS   It's a green colour, the pain. An old green.

SANDRA   Her pain doesn't have a colour any more.

DOUGLAS   I'm talking about me.

SANDRA   She loves you, still.

DOUGLAS   *(Pause)* You think?

Scene Fifteen: Coffee shop

[*Sound/biz:Clatter of cutlery, small talk in booths.*]

ALBERT   Vultures.

VERA   Who?

ALBERT   Those TV people.

ELEANOR   Today's judgement day. They hand down the
          verdict. That's why they're hovering like flies.

ALBERT   They've been swarming all week, trying to make
          something out of nothing.

ELDON   C'mon, now. Tina wasn't "nothing."

ALBERT   Did I say that? That's not what I said.

VERA   Yes it is.

ALBERT   It's not what I meant.

ELDON   What did you mean?

ELEANOR   He means Doug Ramsay is a good man and
          doesn't deserve all this....all this...

31

VERA	Attention.
ELEANOR	Thank you.
ALBERT	The press people, they love this kind of thing. This circus. They never knew Tina.
ELEANOR	And they don't know Doug. They'd know he wouldn't. They'd know he wasn't guilty.
ELDON	He admitted he was. Told Craig Pierce right to his face.
ALBERT	Just 'cause he did it doesn't mean he's guilty.
VERA	Then what does "guilty" mean?
ALBERT	I don't know the law. I know Doug. He did the right thing. He did what was best.
ELDON	Best for who?
ALBERT	Who's side are you on?
ELEANOR	He's playing devil's advocate.
ALBERT	The devil doesn't need an advocate. He's got those press people working for him full-time.
VERA	They're just doing their job.
ALBERT	If they'd stayed away this whole thing would've blown over real quick. They turned this town into a coast-to-coast courtroom. The whole country's one big jury.
ELEANOR	I half-expect to see Keith on television any day now. I'm surprised they haven't done a story about him yet.
ALBERT	Keith isn't news. Keith is slow.

VERA   He's been up on that tower all week, like some frightened bird. That's news.

ELDON   What's he afraid of?

VERA   Maybe he wants to set a record or something.

ALBERT   Don't waste your time trying to understand Keith. Keith is Keith. Doug's the one on trial. He's the one who's innocent. *(Beat)* No one understands that. No one cares.

ELEANOR   He used to feed Tina by hand. Like a baby.

SANDRA   *(Testimony/reverb)* Her food all had to be blended with no lumps in it.

ELEANOR   Poor thing couldn't so much as hold a spoon.

ELDON   How does a devoted father turn around and do what he did?

ALBERT   You playing devil's advocate again?

ELDON   I'm thinking out loud.

VERA   He loved her.

ALBERT   Like nothing else.

ELDON   I know he loved her.

ALBERT   Since when does being a loving father make you a criminal?

ELEANOR   People do funny things `cause of love.

Scene Sixteen: Courthouse steps

[*Sound/biz: A quick refrain of the melee that greeted Doug on the first day of the trial: a media frenzy as reporters swarm around Doug Ramsay, shoving and shouting.*]

REPORTER 1   Was justice done?

[*Sound: The word "justice" reverberates in a rapid succession of different inflections: a statement, a plea, a question, a sneer, and finally, a whisper.*]

Scene Seventeen: Cpl. Pierce's patrol car

[*Sound/biz: The media swarm, quickly muffled as...*
Sound: Car door is slammed.
Sound: Engine is revved. Car drives off.]

PIERCE   I guess you won't be missing them anytime soon.

DOUGLAS   *(Pause)* No.

PIERCE   I guess they're just doing their job.

[*He waits for Doug to respond. Doug remains silent.*]

Listen. Before I take you to. I know I shouldn't be doing this, but I. I know it's wrong. You know Keith has had a bad reaction to all this. I guess you know that. Do you know about the rifle? *(Pause)* Maybe you don't. He had a rifle with him when he first went up the tower. Took a couple of shots at me. *(Nervous laughter)* He doesn't have the gun anymore. Swapped it for food. You know what Keith's appetite is like. He won't come down. He. I was thinking you should have a talk with him. You're the only one. Maybe now that the trial is over he'll listen to you. You get along real well. What d'you think? I can't force you or anything. I mean, I shouldn't even be. I thought it's something you'd want to do. *(Beat)* Do you?

Scene Eighteen: Fire tower

[*Sound: Birds circling above tower. Strong wind. Continues under:*
Sound: Doug's grunts as he climbs up last rungs of tower. He steps onto platform.]

KEITH   You?..

[*Sound: Doug collapses on platform, exhausted from climb.*]

KEITH   You're here.

DOUGLAS   *(Catching breath)* Me. You getting enough to eat?

KEITH   I knew you didn't do it.

DOUGLAS   It's cold up here.

KEITH   You loved her too much.

DOUGLAS   That sleeping bag enough?

KEITH   I knew you'd come up here.

DOUGLAS   What's that?

KEITH   What does it look like?

DOUGLAS   A horse.

KEITH   For Tina. I carved it myself. Tina loves horses.

DOUGLAS   You shouldn't have done that.

KEITH   You don't like it?

DOUGLAS   You shouldn't have carved right into the railing like that.

KEITH   They can fix it. They can put in new wood. From Gordie's lumberyard. *(Beat)* You want a biscuit?

DOUGLAS   I'm not hungry.

KEITH   Some juice.

DOUGLAS   I can't stay.

KEITH   Too cold for you?

DOUGLAS   No.

KEITH   Remember that time I built a fire up here?

DOUGLAS   Keith, you can't stay up here, either.

KEITH   *(Laughing)* A fire on a fire tower.

DOUGLAS   They're waiting for us down below.

KEITH   I wasn't scared.

DOUGLAS   I promised Cpl. Pierce we'd come down together.

KEITH   Tell him to go away.

DOUGLAS   I can't do that.

KEITH   Tell him this is my tower.

DOUGLAS   When we get down, he'll take you home.

KEITH   Tell him to leave us alone.

DOUGLAS	He has a job to do.
KEITH	You'll drive me home.
DOUGLAS	I can't do that.
KEITH	*(Peers over tower)* Where's your truck?
DOUGLAS	They're taking me away, Keith.
KEITH	Away?
DOUGLAS	Prison.
KEITH	*(Pause)* No, no.
DOUGLAS	Yes.
KEITH	No, no, no, no.
DOUGLAS	Yes.
KEITH	You didn't do it.
DOUGLAS	That's not how they saw it.
KEITH	Who?
DOUGLAS	The jury. They announced the verdict this morning.
KEITH	Tina. Tina, Tina. Tinatinatina.
DOUGLAS	She's not in pain. Not anymore.

Scene Nineteen: Court (flashback)

BARCLAY	How much involvement did Douglas have in Tina's day-to-day care?
SANDRA	Lots. When he was home I never had to lift her.

37

He would lift her. When she got home I would give her a drink and then he would lift her from her wheelchair to the couch or wherever she had to go. He did all the bathing. Especially the last year of her life. I was pregnant and I couldn't lift her so he'd bath her. I bathed her once in October but I think the rest of the time that year he did all the bathing. If she threw up, he would – he would clean her up. He would bath her. He changed her diapers, wet or dirty. He was — he was just there for her.

[*Pause.*]

SANDRA   (*Testimony/reverb*) Her muscles were very, very tight and it was starting to twist her body, twist it very badly. They cut a lot of muscles, like her toes, her heel chords, the outside of her knees, abductor muscles. They put her in a body cast so that her back – it was to try and keep these muscles, like from not tightening up, like to try and keep them loose.

Scene Twenty: Fire tower

[*Sound: A strong, menacing wind.*]

KEITH   She's dead.

DOUGLAS   She went to sleep and she never woke up.

KEITH   She. She wasn't a dog.

DOUGLAS   No, she wasn't.

KEITH   She was your daughter.

DOUGLAS   She still is.

KEITH   She was my friend.

DOUGLAS I know.

KEITH You killed her like she was a dog. It's what you do to dogs. You put them to sleep.

CHISHOLM *(Reverb/courtroom)* It is not open season on the disabled.

DOUGLAS She died peacefully.

KEITH How do you know? How do you know how she was feeling? *(Beat)* How do you know?

DOUGLAS I held her in my arms.

KEITH Did you ask her?

DOUGLAS Ask her what?

KEITH If she wanted to die.

DOUGLAS She couldn't speak. You know that.

KEITH She could laugh.

SANDRA *(Testimony/reverb)* She liked to watch bonfires. She liked to see things that moved. Like, if we were in the car and the windshield wipers were going, that would make her laugh when she was well, like when she was younger.

KEITH She laughed when I gave her the mourning dove. Remember? Remember?

[*Sound: Wind fades.*]

DOUG *(Reverb)* Tina, there's someone here to see you. Keith. You know Keith.

KEITH *(Reverb)* This is for you. For your birthday. A mourning dove. To wake you up in the morning. See? *(Beat)* She smiled. She's smiling at me. *(Beat)* If you move the dove up and down, you can pretend it's flying. See?

[*Sound: (Reverb) Tina's laughter.*]

KEITH   *(Reverb)* She's laughing. She likes it. She's laughing.

[*Sound: Tina's laughter cross-fades with wind blowing across fire tower.*]

DOUGLAS   She used to laugh. When she was younger.

Scene Twenty-one: Court (flashback)

CHISHOLM   We submit that the Accused is guilty beyond any reasonable doubt of the first degree murder of his daughter. Now, while Tina may have been frail medically, she was fit enough for surgery and indeed there was an impending surgery coming. Before I go further, I just want to read to you one from the 12 Commandments for Parents of Children with Disabilities and it's just the first commandment. "Thou art thy child's best and most consistent advocate." I certainly suggest that is not what happened here. When we speak about Tina Ramsay, I'm sure the first thoughts that run through everyone's mind is that she was indeed very frail, a 38-pound, 12-year-old girl, couldn't walk, couldn't talk, who was totally dependent on everybody for all that she needed in life, and Sandra Ramsay certainly stressed that in fact Tina had seizures every day of her life. Almost everyone involved in this case seems to portray or suggest that Tina's was a very dreadful existence but I suggest that's simply not so. As Sandra said, Tina liked to sit outside. She liked to watch a fire, and which one of us doesn't like to sit there and watch a fire and think all kinds of thoughts. She would laugh at windshield wipers on the car. She would smile whenever she saw other members of her family because she recognized them all. She could laugh, she could smile, she could cry. What more, for her, did there need to be? Her care was no different than what you would give to one of your babies and indeed, it's no worse, just different. As Sandra put it, Tina was like a two or three-month-old baby and I suggest to you that your decision should be no different here in this case than it would be if the Accused had murdered a baby. Why should it be any different?

Scene Twenty-two: Fire tower

[*Sound: Strong wind.*]

KEITH   Maybe she wanted to live.

DOUGLAS   They were going to operate again. Cut off part of a bone. But the pain wouldn't've stopped. That's no way to live.

KEITH   How do you know what she wanted? You're not God.

DOUGLAS   I'm her father.

KEITH   Not the same.

DOUGLAS   If she'd cried in the truck, I would've taken her out.

KEITH   God decides when it's time.

DOUGLAS   She never cried.

KEITH   God's will.

DOUGLAS   I would never hurt her.

41

KEITH	My granny says that all the time. God's will.
DOUGLAS	Your granny didn't have seizures. Seizures, seizures, all day long.
KEITH	God's will.
DOUGLAS	Stainless steel rods in her back.
KEITH	I know someone with a steel plate in his head.
DOUGLAS	He isn't Tina. Tina is Tina.
KEITH	Tina is dead.
DOUGLAS	Tina never had a chance. Not a fair one.
SANDRA	*(Testimony/reverb)* When she was little I cried myself to sleep every night for a year. That's when I grieved. I did all my grieving when she was little. We lost her then.
KEITH	What you did wasn't fair.
DOUGLAS	Don't tell me about fair and unfair. I lived with unfair every day of her life.

Scene Twenty-three: Court (flashback)

BARCLAY	All of the medical personnel emphasized that Tina's parents were in the best position to try and interpret what was going on in Tina's body and in her mind. They were in the best position to assess the pain that she was in and in fact throughout Tina's life Douglas and Sandra Ramsay made every single decision that was ever made by Tina. They decided whether she would eat, what she would eat, how much she would eat. They decided whether she would roll over, whether she would sit up, whether she would have a clean diaper, whether or not – even

whether or not she would have a bowel movement. I suggest no one was in a better position than Doug and Sandra Ramsay to understand what kind of pain their daughter was in and even those who didn't know Tina perceived her to be in excruciating pain.

Scene Twenty-four: Fire tower

KEITH   I'm not going down.

DOUGLAS   You can't stay here.

KEITH   I like it here. Safe. *(Beat)* Safe.

DOUGLAS   It's safer down there.

KEITH   Not for me.

DOUGLAS   Why not?

KEITH   Not for people like me.

DOUGLAS   What are you afraid of?

               [*Keith doesn't reply.*]

DOUGLAS   What are you afraid of?

KEITH   *(Pause)* You.

DOUGLAS   Me?

KEITH   You.

DOUGLAS   Why me?

KEITH   *(Pause)* Are you going to kill me, too?

DOUGLAS   *(Emotionally winded)* What?

KEITH	Like you killed Tina.
DOUGLAS	I would never hurt you.
KEITH	You killed Tina. We're the same.
DOUGLAS	You're not the same.
KEITH	Same, same.
DOUGLAS	Not true.
KEITH	Same because we're different.
DOUGLAS	Tina had severe cerebral palsy. You –
KEITH	I've got Down's.
DOUGLAS	You can't compare. It's two different – You don't understand.
KEITH	*You* don't understand.
DOUGLAS	Tina was my daughter. You're my friend.
KEITH	A freak.
DOUGLAS	You're not a freak.
KEITH	Some people say so. A freak of nature. Like Tina.
DOUGLAS	You're not Tina.
KEITH	You killed her because she was different.
DOUGLAS	Because of the pain.
KEITH	Pain made her different. If she had no pain, she wouldn't be different. You wouldn't have killed her.
DOUGLAS	She was suffering.

KEITH   You don't kill something because it's different. It's not right. That's what my granny says.

DOUGLAS   I wasn't thinking of you when...

KEITH   When you killed Tina. *(Beat)* When are you going to kill me?

DOUGLAS   I'm not going to kill you.

KEITH   How do I know?

DOUGLAS   Keith...

KEITH   How do I know?

DOUGLAS   I'm not like that.

KEITH   Tina didn't know you were going to kill her.

DOUGLAS   She couldn't understand.

KEITH   She couldn't protect herself.

           [*Doug steps forward.*]

KEITH   Stay away.

DOUGLAS   I'm not going to hurt you.

KEITH   Don't touch me.

DOUGLAS   We can climb down the tower together.

KEITH   I'm staying. I'm safe.

DOUGLAS   You're safe down there.

KEITH   Stand back.

           [*Sound/biz: Doug steps forward to comfort Keith. Keith misinterprets the gesture. They struggle briefly. Keith begins to cry.*]

KEITH   Don't kill me. Please don't kill me.

Scene Twenty-five: Court: duelling lawyers (flashback)

BARCLAY   I urge you, when you look at this case, to look at it and say, what is the right thing to do in this case?

CHISHOLM   What gives Douglas Ramsay the right to wipe out potentially the next 30 years of Tina's life?

BARCLAY   If my client has committed a sin against God, God will judge him.

CHISHOLM   This is but one man's abhorrent decision because he no longer valued Tina's life as he did that of his other children.

BARCLAY   The only thing we're here to deal with today is whether or not the highest legal sanction known to Canadian law should apply to Douglas Ramsay. Should he be categorized as a first degree murderer?

CHISHOLM   I can only state that this was a murder most foul, callous, cold, calculating, heartless and not motivated by anything other than making his own life easier.

BARCLAY   I don't wish any of you to get the idea that in any way this trial is anything more than the trial of the guilt or innocence of Douglas Ramsay.

CHISHOLM   So the question arises, what is or what was Douglas Ramsay's cause, and I use that phrase because in an interview he said he wasn't taking up anyone else's cause, so what was his cause?

BARCLAY	This is not a cause. This isn't going to start some slippery slope argument that you need be worried about.
CHISHOLM	Are we saying that those who wish or care for us can determine our fate?
BARCLAY	Nothing about this case *per se* legalizes euthanasia.
CHISHOLM	Does the philosophy become: "Since we brought you into this world we can decide when you leave?"
BARCLAY	You only have to deal with this set of facts.
CHISHOLM	I would simply ask you just to remember and look at photo 32 in Exhibit P-1 of Tina. Think of her. Just for a moment.
BARCLAY	You only have to deal with what's the right thing in this set of facts.
CHISHOLM	She had presence.
BARCLAY	We only need to be concerned here about the justice of this case and whether or not your conscience would feel right in sending this man away with a conviction for first degree murder.
CHISHOLM	She had the right to live.

Scene Twenty-six: Fire tower

KEITH	*(Crying; frightened)* I don't want to die.
DOUGLAS	I don't want you to die.
KEITH	Don't do to me what you did to Tina.
DOUGLAS	No.

KEITH   Just because I'm different.

DOUGLAS   No.

KEITH   I'm scared.

DOUGLAS   I'm holding you.

KEITH   Don't hurt me.

DOUGLAS   Never.

KEITH   You hurt her.

DOUGLAS   I didn't see it like that.

KEITH   You hurt me.

DOUGLAS   I see that now.

KEITH   *(Cries)* Tina. Tinatinatina.

[*Wipes his nose, sniffles.*]

Why're you crying?

Scene Twenty-seven: Court (flashback)

JUDGE   There is no joy in this for anyone. I know you believe you did the right thing and many people will agree with it; however, the criminal law is unremitting when it comes to the taking of human life for whatever reason. Life was not kind to Tina but it was a life that was hers to make of what she could. I am left with no option but to order that you be sentenced to imprisonment for life without eligibility for parole until you have served ten years of the sentence. Mr. Ramsay, is there anything you want to say?

DOUGLAS   I still feel I did what was right.

JUDGE   Yes, anything else?

DOUGLAS   Well, my wife mentioned that it's not a crime to cut her leg off, not a crime to stick a feeding tube in her stomach, not a crime to let her lay there in pain for another 20 years. I don't think – I don't think you people are being human.

Scene Twenty-eight: Fire tower

PIERCE   *(Off; from below tower)* Doug? *(Beat)* Doug, what's happening up there?

DOUGLAS   We're coming down.

KEITH   What about the horse?

DOUGLAS   Horse?

KEITH   The horse I carved for Tina.

DOUGLAS   Let's leave it here. She would've liked it up here.

KEITH   She loved watching fires.

DOUGLAS   *(Pause)* She did.

KEITH   You wanna go down first?

DOUGLAS   You go. I'll follow.

END

Denial is a River

Denial is a River was first broadcast on *Morningside* on September 4, 1996 with the following cast:

HANNAH KANE	Susan Hogan
BRUCE KANE	Michael Hogan
DR. HASTINGS	Gordon Pinsent
DODI	Patricia Vanstone
MAGGIE	Danielle Brett
GILLIAN	Catherine Disher
ANITA SAUREN	Lally Cadeau
CLINIC TECHNICIAN	Mung-Ling Tsui
ROBSON	Geoffrey Bowes
RECEPTIONIST	Kathryn Miller
DR. SIMMS	Megan Smith
SANGFROID	Martin Julien
STREET PUNK	Lawrence Bayne

Producer	Gregory J. Sinclair
Recording Engineer	Greg DeClute
Sound Effects	Greg DeClute
	John Stewart
Production Assistant	Nina Callaghan
Casting Director	Linda Grearson

Scene One

HANNAH   My name is Hannah Kane. I am 56 years old. For thirty-one years I was married to Bruce Kane. For twenty-four years I taught English at Woodruff Heights Secondary School. For five years I have had AIDS. I have two beautiful daughters, Maggie and Gillian. I write these words for the sake of my children, and my children's children; Ashley, Ryan, and Claire. The day will come when my grandchildren will wonder why their grandparents died at such a young age. My husband died when he was fifty-four. I am dying. I am making my story public to try and prevent what could have — should have — been prevented. My life for the past five years has been an endless stream of could haves, should haves. Most days, I rewrite the past. I imagine I am somewhere I have never been. I confront those I never confronted, including myself. Let my words survive long after I'm gone. One day soon, the sea will carry my ashes. My story begins and ends with the sea. That is where Bruce and I met for the first time. On a hot summer day by the sea in Nova Scotia. He saved a young boy's life, and mine.

Scene Two: Seaside beach — flashback

[*Sound/biz: Crashing waves, seagulls, sunbathers and swimmers frolicking on beach and on sand. Continues under:*]

HANNAH   (*Narration*) I was nineteen years old, walking along the beach with Dodi MacLean, my girlfriend since I was seven. Dodi noticed it first. A young boy, splashing and thrashing, waving his arms.

DODI   Hannah, look. Out there.

HANNAH   Where?

DODI   Past the raft. See? Someone's...Look, he keeps struggling to...Oh, God, he's drowning. Look! Help him! *(Shouting to anyone and everyone)* He's drowning! Help him. Please. Somebody!

          [*Sound/biz: Crowd reacts to Dodi's cries: children scream, parents call out for their children. One mother's voice surfaces, a hysterical voice calling out her son's name: Stephen.*]

HANNAH   *(Narration)* Everyone watched as Bruce swam out to the drowning boy, as determined as a dog paddling towards a stick. The boy was a limp sack in his arms. The crowd parted. Bruce dropped to his knees and lay the boy on the sand.

MOTHER   He's dead!!

BYSTANDER He ain't dead. Not yet.

          [*The bystander is shushed by the crowd.*]

HANNAH   Who is he?

DODI   Who knows. Some local kid.

HANNAH   Not the boy. *Him.*

DODI   Oh, him.

HANNAH   Where's he from?

DODI   Not here. We would have noticed.

HANNAH   *(Narration)* Bruce was hunched over the boy, mouth-to-mouth. Everyone watched and waited.

          [*Sound: Young boy coughs, spits up water.*]

[*Sound/biz: Mother's cry of relief; murmurs of approval; an excited buzz; various crowd comments: "Call a doctor; he doesn't need one; he shouldn't've been swimming that far out; if he was my boy, I'd clip him one."*]

HANNAH   Where'd he go?

DODI   Who?

HANNAH   He was just here. He disappeared. *(Beat)* Wait. Over there!

DODI   Where are you going?

HANNAH   *(Running off)* I'll catch up with you later.

DODI   *(Yelling)* Hannah! Hannah!

[*Sound:Crashing waves up and under:*]

HANNAH   *(Catching up)* Hey! Mr. Hero!

BRUCE   I'm not a hero.

HANNAH   You're too modest.

BRUCE   Too modest is better than one.

HANNAH   What?

BRUCE   Never mind.

HANNAH   Where're you going?

BRUCE   *(Off)* For a swim.

HANNAH   Can I join you?

BRUCE   *(Off)* Swim at your own risk.

HANNAH   Looks like I'm in safe company.

BRUCE   *(Off)* Think or swim.

[*Sound: Crashing waves under:*]

Scene Three

HANNAH   That's where we were married. By the sea, on a clear August day in 1959. Bruce wanted to yell our vows, loud enough, he said, to wake up his ancestors buried in Ireland. It was his Irish blood that hooked me. His puckish sense of humour. His silly word games. His love for music, and a good drink. He was a leprechaun in another life, I'm sure of it. He had flaming red hair, and a temper to match. Blue eyes. Broad shoulders. Large hands so delicate, they could pluck fallen eyelashes off my cheek.

Scene Four: Hearing — academy of physicians

COMMITTEE CHAIR   We are here today in the matter of a Hearing directed by the Complaints Committee of the Royal Academy of Physicians and Surgeons between the academy and Dr. Hastings. Dr. Hastings has been charged with professional misconduct for failure to maintain the standard of practice of the profession in respect to his treatment of his patient, the complainant's husband, now deceased. He has also been charged with professional misconduct for an act relevant to the practice of medicine that, having regard to all the circumstances, would reasonably be regarded by members as disgraceful, dishonourable and unprofessional. Ms. Sauren, you may begin.

SAUREN   Dr. Hastings, you have been a family physician for how long now?

HASTINGS   Thirty-seven years.

SAUREN   And Bruce Kane was a patient of yours.

HASTINGS   Yes.

SAUREN   For how many years?

HASTINGS   Almost thirty.

SAUREN   Over the course of those thirty years, would it be fair to say you had a good physician-patient relationship?

HASTINGS   Oh, yes. Very good. Excellent.

Scene Five: The Kanes' dining room

[*Sound: Easy listening music. Continues under:*]

BRUCE   Ta-dah!

HANNAH   What's that? You're not allowed to drink.

BRUCE   This, my dear, is non-alcoholic. So am I. I want to celebrate.

HANNAH   Celebrate?

BRUCE   My successful operation.

HANNAH   You haven't had it yet.

BRUCE   I'll be too drowsy afterwards. You know what I'm like. I want to celebrate now. *(Beat)* What's wrong?

HANNAH   Nothing's wrong.

BRUCE   You're wearing your "Something's wrong" face.

HANNAH   Nothing is wrong.

BRUCE   If nothing was wrong you'd be wearing your "Nothing's wrong" face. I know your "Nothing's wrong" face, and this isn't it. *(Beat)* You're worried.

HANNAH   I'm not worried.

BRUCE   You're wearing your "worried" glasses.

HANNAH   I'm wearing contacts.

BRUCE   When you wear your "worried" glasses on your "Something's wrong" face, then I know you're heading for some major fretting. Didn't you major in fretting at university?

[*Sound: Hannah playfully hits Bruce with a couch pillow.*]

HANNAH   Stop it.

BRUCE   A major in fretting with a minor in pillow fighting. That's why I married you.

[*Sound: A playful pillow fight between them. Bruce begins to cough.*]

HANNAH   Careful. *(Beat)* You're frightened.

BRUCE   Frightened? *Moi?* I'm the King of Cardiac Surgery. Four operations in the last two years. Long live the king!

[*Sound: Bruce shakes bottle; cork pops out.*]

HANNAH   Bruce! The carpet!

BRUCE   It won't stain.

HANNAH   You always do this. You, you get into this, this heightened state of denial.

Denial is a River

BRUCE   Denial is a river.

HANNAH   Please! No word games. Not now. Honestly, some days I wish you'd be as, as depressed and frightened and scared as anyone else who's going through what...Going through what we're going through.

BRUCE   Repeat after me "Reoperative bypass."

HANNAH   Stop it.

BRUCE   I'll be fine, Hannah. We'll be fine.

HANNAH   I hope so.

BRUCE   I'm the King of Cardiac Surgery. Long live the king! *(Pause; Hannah doesn't respond)* Long live the king!

HANNAH   *(Pause)* Long live the king.

Scene Six: Hearing — academy of physicians

SAUREN   Would it be fair to say that during the three decades or so during which Bruce Kane was your patient he came to trust you?

HASTINGS   All my patients trust me.

Scene Seven: Hospital — intensive care unit

[*Sound/biz: Heart monitor; P.A. System in background, paging doctors, etc. Fades and continues under:*]

INTERN   Kane. Bruce. *(Pause)* He's had better days.

NURSE   And nights. Cardiac arrest during the operation. Internal bleeding.

INTERN   Cryoprecipitate will stem the bleeding. Give him eight to ten units.

[*Sound: Heart monitor, up and out.*]

Scene Eight

HANNAH   Cryoprecipitate. I have said that word a thousand times. I've chewed on it for days on end, like a dog with a bone. I've defined it for friends, family, strangers. "A fluffy white protein mass that's extracted from blood and helps clotting." Fluffy and white sounds so, so cozy. Fluffy and white, like a cloud. Like cotton. Like fresh snow. The cryoprecipitate that was injected into Bruce the morning after his operation was extracted from the blood of a man who had his own story to tell, if he could. He's dead, too. But two months before Bruce's operation, he was very much alive. I don't know his name. I call him Mr. Sangfroid. That's French for "cold blood." Forgive me. My French is as bad as my husband's. Mr. Sangfroid was feeling so full of life, he decided to donate some blood. For the sake of those who needed it. For the sake of people like my husband.

Scene Nine: Blood donors' clinic

[*Sound/biz: The hum of a clinic.*]

TECHNICIAN   Have you given blood before?

SANGFROID   Once a year, every year.

TECH   Then you know what to expect. You read the pamphlet.

SANGFROID   Backwards and forwards.

HANNAH:	He can't read.
TECH	I beg your pardon?
HANNAH:	Before you ask him if he's read the pamphlet why don't you ask him if he can read?
TECH	This is a clinic for blood donors, not a literacy class for immigrants. *(To Sangfroid)* I'm going to prick your finger for type and hemogloblin level. *(Beat)* Done.
SANGFROID	Painless.
TECH	Here's a questionnaire for you to fill in —
HANNAH:	Nothing about AIDS.
TECH	I beg your pardon?
HANNAH:	Your questionnaire doesn't ask anything about AIDS. *(To Sangfroid)* You haven't heard about AIDS, have you?
SANGFROID	AIDS?
HANNAH:	No questions about unprotected sex. You've had unprotected sex with many partners, haven't you?
SANGFROID	I get lonely.
HANNAH:	Male and female partners.
SANGFROID	I'm not gay, if that's what you're thinking. Lonely is lonely. Sex is sex.
HANNAH:	*(To technician)* And what's your excuse?
TECH	Excuse me?
HANNAH:	He hasn't heard of AIDS. He's not in the blood

business. You are. Why aren't you testing for AIDS?

TECH   The odds of blood being infected with the AIDS virus is one in a million.

HANNAH: What in God's name are you talking about? Who gave you these odds?

TECH   Our medical experts. You have as great a chance of getting AIDS from blood as getting cancer from smoking one single cigarette.

HANNAH: Lift your head out of the sand!

SANGFROID   Listen, I'm strong as a horse.

HANNAH: You listen! The blood you give today will kill my husband five years from now.

TECH   I'm going to have to ask you to leave.

HANNAH: You have a responsibility. Ask him about AIDS. Test his blood. Now. Not a year from now. Do it. Before his blood kills my husband. Before it kills me. Please.

TECH   It's time you left.

SANGFROID   What about me?

TECH   A nurse will be with you shortly.

Scene Ten

HANNAH   Mr. Sangfroid donated his bad blood in November 1984. Two months later it was swimming in Bruce's body. It took another year before they tested blood donors for AIDS.

Scene Eleven: Hearing

SAUREN   Dr. Hastings, in April 1989 you received a phone call from Dr. Walsh, Haemotologist-in-Charge of the blood transfusion laboratory at Peel Memorial Hospital, where Bruce Kane's cardiac surgery took place in December 1984.

HASTINGS   That is correct.

SAUREN   What was the thrust of your telephone conversation with Dr. Walsh?

HASTINGS   He told me that Mr. Kane had received a transfusion that was likely contaminated with AIDS. Mr. Kane had been identified as having received blood or blood products donated by an individual who had eventually tested HIV positive.

SAUREN   So the donated blood, or blood products, which Bruce Kane received during cardiac surgery in December 1984 was HIV positive?

HASTINGS   Dr. Walsh didn't know if the blood received by Bruce Kane was contaminated. The HIV status of the unit Mr. Kane received was unknown. Dr. Walsh said there was a *likelihood* the blood was contaminated.

SAUREN   And you discussed this likelihood with Dr. Walsh.

HASTINGS   I did. Yes.

HANNAH: Why didn't you discuss it with my husband?

SAUREN   And what conclusions did you reach?

HASTINGS   We didn't reach any conclusions. It was a discussion, not a debate. This was four and a half years after Mr. Kane's operation. He did not look like someone with AIDS. If you know

63

what I mean. He had none of the signs. I didn't believe an effective treatment existed for AIDS-infected patients who didn't show any signs of the disease.

SAUREN   Is it true that you had not previously cared for a patient with HIV infection?

HASTINGS   I read up on it in medical journals. I attended a conference on AIDS for family physicians. I had conversations with my colleagues. We would discuss these matters over coffee.

HANNAH: Over coffee?

SAUREN   You knew that AIDS could become manifest even after five years from HIV seroconversion, that in April 1989 Mr. Kane could have been infected from his operation in December 1984 but not yet shown it?

HASTINGS   It was possible. As I said, I discussed the issue with some colleagues.

SAUREN   Did you consult the specialist in infectious disease at Peel Memorial?

HASTINGS   I did not. No.

SAUREN   Did you notify the Medical Officer of Health of your patient's possible HIV infection.

HASTINGS   No.

SAUREN   So, effectively, you did nothing with the information that Dr. Walsh shared with you during that telephone conversation in April 1989.

HASTINGS   I wrote it down on a Post-it.

HANNAH: A Post-it?

SAUREN   Those small, sticky pieces of paper you scribble on and stick to telephones and whatnot?

HASTINGS   I don't stick them on whatnot.

SAUREN   Where did you put the Post-it with the information that, in all likelihood, Bruce Kane had been contaminated with HIV-infected blood?

HASTINGS   I placed it in his medical file and awaited a letter of confirmation from Dr. Walsh.

SAUREN   Did that letter of confirmation ever arrive?

HASTINGS   No.

HANNAH: Why didn't you call him back when you hadn't heard from him? Why didn't you follow it up? What were you waiting for?

SAUREN   And the Post-it, Dr. Hastings? Do you still have it?

HASTINGS   No. They are not meant to be saved.

Scene Twelve: Hastings' office

HASTINGS   Breathe in.

                [*Sound: Bruce inhales/exhales.*]

HASTINGS   Again.

BRUCE   *(Listless)* I don't get it. We're closing in on five years since the operation. Other men who've had the same surgery, they look great. How come I feel so lousy?

HASTINGS   Other men didn't lose their companies.

BRUCE   I didn't *lose* my company. I sold it.

HASTINGS   Yes, well. Perhaps. Nasty business any way you look at it. You need an awfully thick skin.

BRUCE   I can handle the stress. Why can't I shake this flu?

HANNAH   He's been complaining for months.

HASTINGS   You're not made of steel. You've been through a lot. Take a vacation. You and the missus.

HANNAH   My name is Hannah.

HASTINGS   You and Hannah.

BRUCE   So it's not serious. Nothing to worry about?

HANNAH   He needs reassurance.   .

HASTINGS   He needs a holiday. Doctor's orders.

Scene Thirteen

HANNAH   We followed Dr. Hastings' orders and took a trip to the Bahamas. It was Christmas, 1989, five years after Bruce's operation. On days when I rewrite history, I spend a lot of time going over our Bahamas trip.

Scene Fourteen: Bahamian beach

[*Sound: Caribbean splendour: crashing waves, birds, tourists frolicking on beach and in water. Continues under:*]

HANNAH   Wake up, sleepy-head.

BRUCE   You're getting me wet!

HANNAH   Salt water. It's good for the bones. What are you always telling the kids? Better than chicken soup, and easier to swim in. Come on, let's go for a walk.

BRUCE | I'm too tired.

[*He coughs — a dry, hacking cough that punctuates the conversation.*]

HANNAH | You've been sleeping all day. You could use the exercise.

BRUCE | I don't want exercise. I want to sleep.

HANNAH: | Let him sleep.

HANNAH | We didn't book a week in the Bahamas so you could sleep. Let's go out for dinner.

BRUCE | I'm not hungry.

HANNAH | You're not hungry. You feel exhausted. You've got a pain in your legs. You're a regular barrel of laughs.

HANNAH: | Easy, Hannah.

BRUCE | I can't shake the runs.

HANNAH | A lot of people get the runs on holiday. What you've got is —

BRUCE | Is what?

HANNAH: | Don't say it.

HANNAH | What you've got is more in your mind than anywhere else.

BRUCE | This rash is not a figment of my imagination.

HANNAH: | He's right.

HANNAH	Bruce, it's symptomatic of your depression.
HANNAH:	Stop it. Stop doing this to him.
BRUCE	I didn't know you had a medical degree.
HANNAH	You don't need to be a doctor to see what I see. I saw a grown man build a blue chip ad agency from scratch, only to see it swallowed by a competitor who doesn't even have the grace to ease you out the door. They drop you off the eighteenth floor and wish you a pleasant flight. I'd have a rash on my chest and arms and God knows where else if I'd been through what you've been through. But, Bruce, it's time to get through it. It's time to stop feeling sorry for yourself. *(Pause)* Where are you going?
BRUCE	Back to the room. I don't feel well.
HANNAH:	Let him go.
HANNAH	*(Beat)* Bruce. Bruce!

Scene Fifteen: Kanes' hotel - evening

[*Sound: Gentle lapping of waves in background. Continues under:*]

HANNAH	*(On balcony)* Better get dressed. We're being watched.
BRUCE	*(Off)* By who?
HANNAH	The moon. Come out and see it.
BRUCE	*(Off)* I want to go to bed.
HANNAH	We just went to bed. You were wonderful.
BRUCE	*(Off)* I want to go to sleep.

HANNAH   Come and say goodnight to the moon first.

BRUCE   *(Off)* Hannah...

HANNAH   Please.

BRUCE   *(Steps onto balcony)* Goodnight, moon.

HANNAH   Goodnight comb. And goodnight brush.
                Goodnight nobody. Goodnight mush.

BRUCE   And goodnight to the old lady whispering "hush."

HANNAH   It's Ashley's favourite bedtime story now.
                Maggie reads it to her every night.

BRUCE   If I got a dime for every time I read *Goodnight
                Moon* to Maggie and Gillian, I'd be a rich man.

HANNAH   You *are* a rich man.

                [*Bruce absorbs the thought, the moment.*]

BRUCE   Goodnight stars.

HANNAH   Goodnight air.

BRUCE &
HANNAH   {   Goodnight noises everywhere.

                Scene Sixteen: Hearing

SAUREN   Dr. Hastings, how did you reach the conclusion,
                when you first learned Mr. Kane might be
                infected, that he had been celibate for three
                years and would continue to be celibate
                afterwards? Did you think he would abstain
                forever, that he would never make love with his
                wife again, `til death do they part?

HASTINGS   He was a depressed man, you know.

SAUREN	And depressed men never, ever have sex, is that right?
HASTINGS	My medical records contained a cardiology resident's report from 1983 stating that Mr. Kane was impotent. At a general check-up in December '84 I wrote that Mr. Kane's sexual activity was diminished. Notations made in 1986 and 1988 indicate that there was no sexual activity.
SAUREN	Really? Mr. Kane's impotence would come as a great surprise to Mrs. Kane. She and her husband made love two weeks before Mr. Kane entered hospital for the last time, six weeks before he died due to complications arising from AIDS. How can an impotent man make love, Dr. Hastings?
HASTINGS	I don't know. I wasn't there.
HANNAH:	I was. And we made love, Dr. Hastings, your records be damned. Why didn't you tell Bruce he may have had AIDS?
HASTINGS	I considered it, and decided it wasn't necessary.
HANNAH:	Why not?
HASTINGS	I reviewed his records and concluded your husband and you were not sexually active, and therefore there was no risk of transmission. I didn't want to burden him with bad news.
HANNAH:	You decided the truth would be too much of a burden.
HASTINGS	The truth is, Mrs. Kane, your husband was in no condition to be given such devastating news. He was very emotional and feeling very fragile. To tell a depressed cardiac patient of the possibility that he may have received infected blood posed a severe risk.

HANNAH: The severe risk, Dr. Hastings, was not telling my husband.

HASTINGS I assumed he wasn't having have sexual relations.

HANNAH: You assumed, but you couldn't be certain.

HASTINGS No.

HANNAH: Didn't you have an obligation to discuss the matter with my husband? Didn't you have to be sure, 100 per cent certain, that Bruce wasn't sexually active before deciding not to tell him his blood might have been tainted? Isn't that a physician's responsibility?

HASTINGS Yes.

HANNAH: Then why didn't you discuss it with him? Why didn't you ask him one simple question "Are you having sex?" Were you too embarrassed?

HASTINGS As I explained, Mrs. Kane, I had your husband's best interests at heart.

Scene Seventeen

HANNAH We got back from the Bahamas, and I began to see that Bruce's poor health was not simply a case of mind over matter. It was real, and getting worse. The dry, hacking cough persisted, like a knock at a door that doesn't let up. By the end of February he was in terrible shape. Chills and a high fever that were taking their toll. At the beginning of March, we — my daughters and I — we insisted he go to the hospital. He was too weak to put up a struggle. By the time he was admitted Bruce was suffering from severe shortness of breath, profuse sweating and high fever. As I wheeled him through the hospital doors, he motioned me to bend down and put my ear next to his mouth. "Sugar," he whispered. He always called me Sugar. Sugar Kane. Him and his word games.

BRUCE   *(Reverb)* Sugar, there's a rough river to cross, but I'll meet you on the other side.

HANNAH   Then he kissed me on the cheek. The next day we were told it was pneumonia. Two days later Bruce was transferred to the ICU and immediately put on a ventilator.

[*Sound: Ventilator. Fades and continues under:*]

HANNAH   The weeks that followed were a chronicle of horror for my husband. There were days of seizures and nose bleeds and unspeakable indignities to his body. He wasted away and shrivelled up until all of his major organs except for his heart had stopped functioning. He wasn't responding to antibiotics. There is a daycare at the hospital, for the staff and visitors. That is where we sat, my daughters and I. Ashley and Ryan played with Play-doh while Gillian wondered if her father might be dying of AIDS.

Scene Eighteen: Hospital daycare

[*Sound/biz: Children playing at daycare playground. Continues under:*]

GILLIAN   I'm not saying he has AIDS. I'm saying it's possible.

MAGGIE   Mom, are you listening?

GILLIAN   Leave her. She can hear.

MAGGIE   What are the chances, that, that he actually has it?

GILLIAN   I'm not a doctor.

MAGGIE   I know that! I, I don't understand how this
                could have happened.

GILLIAN   *(To herself)* A prostitute? *(Pause)* I'm sorry. I'm
                thinking out loud, that's all.

MAGGIE   Maybe he was bisexual, too.

GILLIAN   I didn't say that.

MAGGIE   You were thinking it.

GILLIAN   Don't you tell me what I was thinking!

MAGGIE   I'm trying to find some answers. I need your
                help. None of this is making sense.

GILLIAN   He had heart surgery. He lost a lot of blood.

MAGGIE   That was more than five years ago!

GILLIAN   It can take that long for the signs to show up.
                Longer.

MAGGIE   Why weren't we told!

GILLIAN   Ma, say something. Please.

HANNAH   *(Pause)* What do you want me to say? Your
                father is dying. Is he dying of AIDS? I don't
                know. All I know is that he is dying, and that he
                needs us. That's all I know. That's enough.

Scene Nineteen: Hospital

[*Sound/biz: The beep of medical equipment,
doctors being paged, stretchers rolling down
corridors. Continues under:*]

73

HANNAH	I thought…Isn't testing for AIDS standard practice?
DOCTOR	We require the patient's permission.
HANNAH	His permission? My husband is dying. He's too weak to give his permission.
DOCTOR	In this case we would need yours.
HANNAH	Then you have it. Do a blood test. Do whatever it is that you do, but I have a husband to take care of.

Scene Twenty: Bruce Kane's hospital room

[*Sound: Ventilator/life support.*]

HANNAH	*(Narration)* I forgot about the blood test. I spent all my time with Bruce. He was where I wanted to be. He was who I wanted to be with. One morning he tried to write a message but the hands that once lifted me up were too weak to hold a pencil. I bent down and heard him speak for the first time in weeks.
BRUCE	Time to go.
HANNAH	*(Pause)* You want to go?
BRUCE	Enough.
HANNAH	*(Narration)* Before my daughters arrived with their husbands I sat with Bruce. I held his hand, rubbed slow circles with my thumb, hoping against hope that he would turn and tell me one of his stupid word plays. One pun was all I needed to puncture the nightmare.
BRUCE	*(Reverb)* Denial is a river.

HANNAH   *(Reverb)* You plan on taking me dere?

BRUCE   *(Reverb)* De sooner, de better.

HANNAH   *(Narration)* By the time Maggie and Gillian arrived Bruce had been taken off life support.

HANNAH   It's done.

BRUCE   Yes.

HANNAH   *(Narration)* Maggie and Gillian were on either side of him.

MAGGIE   I love you, Daddy.

BRUCE   Yes.

HANNAH   *(Narration)* Gillian couldn't speak. She kissed his fingers instead. I sat on his bed and held him in my arms. I caressed his beautiful red hair. I kissed him on his forehead, on his nose, on his lips. He smiled, closed his eyes, and said,

BRUCE   Goodnight, moon.

Scene Twenty-one: Kanes' home

[*Sound:Phone ringing, picked up.*]

HANNAH   Hello?

RECEPTION   *(Filtered)* Mrs. Kane?

HANNAH   Yes.

REC   *(Filtered)* This is Dr. Hastings' office. Dr. Hastings would like to see you.

HANNAH   What about?

REC	*(Filtered)* Dr. Hastings would prefer discussing it with you in person. Can you come in this afternoon?
	[*Long pause.*]
REC	*(Filtered)* Mrs. Kane?
HANNAH	Yes.
REC	*(Filtered)* Shall we say two o'clock?
HANNAH	No.
REC	*(Filtered)* Three-thirty, then?
HANNAH	Now.

Scene Twenty-two: Dr. Hastings' office

HASTINGS	*(Off)* Hannah? Please come in.
	[*Sound/biz: Hannah walks into inner office; Hastings closes door behind him.*]
HASTINGS	How are you holding up?
HANNAH	Most days I feel like I'm walking under water.
HASTINGS	It's been difficult for all of us. *(Pause)* Hannah, I received the results of Bruce's blood tests. *(Pause)* He tested positive for AIDS. *(Beat)* I don't know what to say. I'm, I'm stunned.
HANNAH	*(Pause)* How long do I have to live?
HASTINGS	You don't understand. These are Bruce's test results.
HANNAH	No. You don't understand. Bruce was my husband.

HASTINGS   You weren't having sexual relations with him, were you? *(Beat)* Hannah?

HANNAH   The Bahamas. At Christmas.

HASTINGS   You must be confused. That was only four months ago.

HANNAH   By the light of the moon.

HASTINGS   According to my records, Bruce wasn't...I should have been told.

Scene Twenty-three: Park

[*Sound: Fountain; pigeons cooing. Continues under:*]

HANNAH   I didn't go home. I didn't cry. I bought a loaf of fresh bread, sat down on a bench by a large fountain, and fed pigeons. I pretended to be normal. If you looked at me, you would have thought, "How nice. A woman feeding pigeons." I wasn't a widow who had just learned her husband had died of AIDS. I wasn't a woman who needed a test for AIDS. I was a woman feeding pigeons. That was all I wanted to be.

Scene Twenty-four: Phone conversation

DODI   *(Filtered)* It's been two months since Hastings told you. What are you waiting for?

HANNAH   I need more time, Dodi.

DODI   What you need is a blood test. Call Hastings. I'll call him for you.

HANNAH   He's not my doctor. I'm with Marion Simms. She's an angel.

Making Waves

DODI (Filtered) Call Dr. Simms.

HANNAH I will. Soon. When I get back.

DODI (Filtered) Where are you going?

HANNAH Nova Scotia. With Maggie and Gillian. To scatter Bruce's ashes.

DODI (Filtered) Nova Scotia in June. I can smell the sea from here. I wish I were in your shoes.

HANNAH No. You don't.

Scene Twenty-five: Seaside beach

[Sound: Waves, seagulls. Continues under:]

HANNAH I love the sea at this time of day.

GILLIAN At this time of morning. It's so early.

MAGGIE It's so beautiful.

HANNAH This was your father's favourite time of day. This was his favourite piece of the sea.

GILLIAN (By rote) This is where he saved a young boy's life.

MAGGIE (By rote) This is where you were married.

HANNAH I'm sorry if I sound like an old record. He always told me this is where he wanted to be when it was time to go. I don't even know how you're supposed to do this. I don't have a lot of experience.

[Starts to laugh and cry.]

HANNAH Do I just pour it into the water?

MAGGIE	I brought some shells.
HANNAH	Shells?
MAGGIE	A shell for each of us, to fill with his ashes. Then we can scatter together.
GILLIAN	I'd like that.
HANNAH	So would he.
	[*Sound: Waves up and out.*]

Scene Twenty-six: Outside Dr. Simms office

GILLIAN	How are you feeling?
HANNAH	Healthy. I feel healthy. And that makes me feel hopeful.
MAGGIE	You look good.
GILLIAN	You look like you need a hand to hold.
HANNAH	I feel like I'm seven years old and need my mother.
MAGGIE	We'll be your mother.
GILLIAN	For a change.

Scene Twenty-seven: Dr. Simms' office

[*Sound: Simms closes office door behind her.*]

DR. SIMMS	Ah...The Kane women. How nice to see you all together again.
GILLIAN	It made my father nervous to see the three of us side by side. He called it the Kane mutiny.

[*She begins to sing the tune of "Chain Gang," a cue for her sister and mother join in.*]

GILLIAN   Boom-boom-boom-boom...

H/M/G   "That's the sound of the girls working on the Kane gang...."

[*All three women begin to laugh. Continues under:*]

DR. SIMMS   I have your results, Hannah.

HANNAH   I tested positive.

HANNAH   I tested positive?

DR. SIMMS   Yes.

Scene Twenty-eight

HANNAH   We went home, my daughters and I, and cried over hot pizza and cold wine. We listened to music. We didn't talk all that much. What do you say? The girls insisted they stay for the night. I insisted they go home, to their families. I wanted time alone. Time to talk to Bruce. Time to collect my thoughts. Time. I wanted to shout and scream. I wanted to break something, as I had been broken. I had to do something. And that night, after the longest day of my life, I did.

Denial is a River

Scene Twenty-nine: Red Cross building

[*Sound/biz: The streetscape of a busy street in
downtown Toronto: streetcars, honking horns,
street people, etc. Continues and fades under:
Sound: The rattle of a can of spray paint being
shaken.
Sound: Spray paint against a wall.*]

STREET PUNK   Aren't you a little old for this shit?

HANNAH   You're never too old. Excuse me. You're in the way of my exclamation mark.

[*Sound: Hannah spray paints her exclamation mark.*]

PUNK   Shame! *(Beat)* What's it mean?

HANNAH   You don't know what "shame" means?

PUNK   Yeah. But why're you tagging this wall with it?

HANNAH   This isn't just any wall.

PUNK   Looks like about a million other walls to me.

HANNAH   Look up. What do you see?

PUNK   Stars.

HANNAH   No. Lower. Over there.

PUNK   A flag. A cross. *(Beat)* The Red Cross.

HANNAH   Bingo. This is their wall. This is my statement. Shame. Shame on them. What happened was shameful.

PUNK   I don't get it.

HANNAH   I'm dying.

PUNK	*(Beat)* No shit.
HANNAH	No shit.

Scene Thirty

HANNAH	The Red Cross was my first choice. I could have spray painted the walls of the hospital that took too long to link Bruce with the contaminated blood. I could have spray painted the walls of my high school.

Scene Thirty-one: High school

[*Sound: (off) students chatting, bell ringing. Continues under:*]

ROBSON	Hannah, do you have a minute?
HANNAH	Sure.

[*Sound: Closes classroom door behind him.*]

ROBSON	Listen, I've been getting some calls from parents who are...concerned. They've been hearing rumours. Gossip. Now they're worried their kid is going to catch AIDS by sitting in the same classroom as you. It's crazy. Some of them want their kids transferred to another class, that kind of thing. I won't hear of it. I just wanted you to know, that's all.
HANNAH	I appreciate it.
ROBSON	How are you feeling?
HANNAH	How do I look?
ROBSON	You've always been a trooper.

HANNAH	You didn't answer my question. How do I look?
ROBSON	*(Pause)* Like you could use some time off.
HANNAH	Is that what you want me to do? Take some time off?
ROBSON	I didn't say that Hannah.
HANNAH	I'm saying it. Do you want me to take some time off?
ROBSON	You do what's best.
HANNAH	What I do best is teach.
ROBSON	Even the best teachers get tired. Why don't you take the rest of the day off, get a good night's sleep.
HANNAH	I'll leave. For good.
ROBSON	I'm not asking you to —
HANNAH	It's what I want to do. I want to travel while I still have the strength. I want to see Paris with an old girlfriend of mine. I want to go up the Eiffel Tower and down the Seine. Have you ever been to Paris?
ROBSON	No.
HANNAH	The city of love. I hear it's beautiful.
ROBSON	So I hear.

Scene Thirty-two: Restaurant

[*Sound/biz: Small talk at tables. Continues under: Sound: Chair scraping as Dodi rises to help Hannah.*]

DODI   Hannah, let me.

HANNAH   It's a cane, Dodi. Not a crutch.

DODI   I know.

[*Sound/biz: They settle in their seats.*]

HANNAH   A gift from the girls. They named it Candy Kane. I prefer "walking stick", but there's no getting around it. It is a cane.

DODI   It's colourful.

HANNAH   It's humiliating. A woman my age shouldn't need a cane.

DODI   Does it help?

HANNAH   Yes. That's what hurts.

DODI   Well, then. Down to business. Let's order. Something decadent.

HANNAH   I can't eat decadent. I can barely eat. I won't bore you with dreadful tales about my digestive problems. You can see it on my face.

DODI   You don't look bad.

[*Sound: Dodi unzips purse.*]

DODI   Voila, Madame.

HANNAH   What's this?

DODI   You mean, "Qu'est-ce que c'est?" Two tickets to Paris. First class. We leave in a week. *(Pause)* What's wrong?

HANNAH   I can't go. Not in the shape I'm in.

DODI   Don't be daft. You look fine. A little thin, but so what? It's not like we'll jog up the Eiffel Tower. You've waited long enough.

HANNAH   I'm not going anywhere. Not anymore, Dodi.

DODI   Oh, Hannah. It doesn't have to be like this.

HANNAH   I tell myself that every day. It didn't have to be like this. I'm just still grateful that you are willing to share a table with me. Last week I was at a party and I was asked not to touch any food. Not that I could eat anything. *(Pause)* I have something to show you.

[*Sound: Hannah unzips purse.*]

DODI   What's this?

HANNAH   You mean, "Qu'est-ce que c'est?" *(Shakes can of spray paint)* C'est le spray paint.

DODI   I can see that. What it's for?

HANNAH   For making statements. For making statements on walls. For making statements on the walls of big, important buildings with red crosses on white flags flapping in the wind.

DODI   That's you! I…I remember seeing the picture in the paper. *(Laughs)* You!?

HANNAH   Moi. The first of every month for the past two years.

DODI   But don't they. Doesn't someone see you?

HANNAH   I do it at night, but they know who I am. What are they going to do? Arrest me? Sue me? It wouldn't look good.

DODI   *(Still laughing)* I don't know what to say.

HANNAH	Say, "I'll write you from Paris."
DODI	Hannah.
HANNAH	Say it.
DODI	*(Pause)* I'll write you from Paris.

Scene Thirty-three: Kanes' house

MAGGIE & GILLIAN {	Surprise!
HANNAH	What's all this?
MAGGIE	Croissants. Brie cheese.
GILLIAN	Baguettes, French wine and Edith Piaf. We are going to Paris.
HANNAH	You two are crazy.
MAGGIE	We take after you.
	[*Sound: Gillian takes out cassette, turns on tape deck.* *Music: Piaf— "Je Ne Regrette Rien." Continues under:*]
GILLIAN	Your living room, Madame, is now the Seine. We leave in five minutes.
HANNAH	I don't know what to say.
MAGGIE	Don't say anything. You cut the baguette, I'll wash the grapes.
GILLIAN	I'll open the wine.
HANNAH	Did Dodi put you up to this?

MAGGIE   *(Off)* It was a committee decision.

GILLIAN   After the Seine we are going to the Jeu de Paumes.

MAGGIE   *(Off)* We have slides of the Best of Impressionism, as curated by the Kane sisters. You'll love it.

HANNAH   Dammit!

GILLIAN   What's wrong?

HANNAH   I cut myself.

GILLIAN   I'll get a Band-aid.

HANNAH   No. Javex.

GILLIAN   Javex?

HANNAH   Under the sink. I have to clean all cuts with bleach. That's what my 'infectious disease specialist' told me. That's what happens when you become a leper. You have to play by new rules. Soap out. Javex in. *(Pause)* I'm sorry. Look at all you've done. I will clean this up and we'll go. The three of us, down the Seine. I'd like that.

                [*Music: Piaf. Up and out.*]

Scene Thirty-four

HANNAH   Paris in my living room was lovely, even if the Impressionist paintings were occasionally out of focus. A few months later Dr. Hastings was found guilty of professional misconduct. His license to practise was suspended for two months. Then the icing; his suspension would be suspended if he agreed to take a course in bio-ethics. I hadn't taught in almost three years, I could barely stand, but I was willing, more than willing, to come out of retirement to teach Dr. Hastings a course in bio-ethics. Oh, yes. I could taste the temptation. My first sweet taste in a very long time.

Scene Thirty-five

[*Sound: School bell.*]

HANNAH   Good morning, class.

HASTINGS   *(Tone of a young school boy)* Good morning, Mrs. Kane.

HANNAH   Are you ready for today's quiz, Dr. Hastings?

HASTINGS   Yes, Mrs. Kane.

HANNAH   Very good. Let us begin. A doctor — let's call him Dr. X — has a patient. Patient Y. One day, Dr. X gets a phone call. He's told Patient Y's blood may have been contaminated with HIV during an operation. Dr. X decides not to tell Patient Y. Is that decision fair to Patient Y? To Patient Y's wife? To Patient Y's children?

HASTINGS   It's not for me to judge.

HANNAH   Oh, but you're a doctor. You make judgements all the time.

HASTINGS   Throughout my career I have been guided by my conscience. It has been my moral compass.

HANNAH   And that compass has never failed you?

HASTINGS   None of us are infallible, Mrs. Kane. We live in an imperfect world.

HANNAH   Indeed we do, doctor. And some live a lot longer in this imperfect world than others. I looked forward to a long life with my husband, searching for perfection. I have seen it, doctor. I have watched my grandson chat for half an hour with a lady bug. Is that not perfection? I have felt my husband reach over and silently wrap his hand around mine at the dinner table, in the garden, in bed, and tell me with one gentle squeeze all I needed to know. Is that not perfection? I have known my daughters to leave a warm bed in the middle of a bitterly cold night and drive across town to comfort one another. That is perfection, Dr. Hastings.

HASTINGS   Yes, I imagine it is.

HANNAH   What you can't imagine is what you have done to me and my family.

HASTINGS   My heart goes out to you and your children.

HANNAH   It's not your heart I wonder about. It is the workings of your mind that will always remain a mystery to me.

HASTINGS   My mind is in perfect working order. This has been an ordeal, I can tell you. I wouldn't wish this on anyone. Fortunately, I came through. As for your husband, I have deep regrets.

HANNAH   Regrets can't resuscitate my husband, Dr. Hastings.

HASTINGS   If I may be frank, Mrs. Kane. I have long felt that someone was needed to shoulder the weight of this so-called scandal. Everyone's trying to wash their hands of this mess and wipe it on me. I resent the way I've been treated.

HANNAH   Don' t lecture me on resentment.

HASTINGS   I am one individual, Mrs. Kane. One small link in the chain of events that lead to your husband's death. I am not the bureaucracy that allowed tainted blood to circulate for far too long before acting. I am not the public health system that lacks proper safeguards. I am not the hospital that should have known better. From the beginning, I acted in your husband's best interests.

HANNAH   What about my interests?

HASTINGS   There are others equally deserving of your wrath.

HANNAH   I wish I knew their names.

Scene Thirty-six

HANNAH   Of course, this never happened. But it should have.

Scene Thirty-seven: Red Cross building

[*Sound/biz: The streetscape of a busy street in downtown Toronto: streetcars, honking horns, street people, etc. Continues under:*]

HANNAH   (*Weak voice: her voice is slow and laboured throughout*) Here. Stop here.

DODI   I don't feel good about this.

HANNAH   You don't have to. You're doing it for my sake, not yours. Remember to give it a good shake. Don't stand too close to the wall. The letters will run.

[*Sound: Dodi shaking can of spray paint.*]

HANNAH   Wait. You don't know what to write.

DODI   "Shame."

HANNAH   No. I want something else this time. Here.

DODI   *(Pause)* Hannah, I can't write this.

HANNAH   I would, but I can't. You have no excuse.

DODI   It...It...

HANNAH   It has to be done. Please.

                [*Sound: Dodi spray paints wall. Continues and fades under:*]

Scene Thirty-eight

HANNAH   I sat in my wheelchair and watched Dodi spray paint two epitaphs on the wall. Bruce Kane. 1936-1990. Hannah Prentiss Kane. 1939-1995.

BRUCE   *(Reverb)* Denial is a river.

HANNAH   Denial is a river. One of Bruce's favourite puns. Which I didn't understand at first.

Scene Thirty-nine: Flashback

HANNAH   What do you mean?

BRUCE   De-Nile is a river. In Egypt. De Nile. De Mississippi. De St. Lawrence. They're all rivers.

HANNAH   Oh, you...

                [*Sound/biz: Hannah reacts to Bruce's pun with playful swats. Fades.*]

Scene Forty

HANNAH   I am dying. I am drowning. All that remains is my story. Do with it what you will. Remember what happened, and why. Remember my name.

END

Past Imperfect

Past Imperfect was first broadcast on *Sunday Showcase* on December 14, 1997 with the following cast:

MICHEL BEAUCHEMIN	Jean-Louis Roux
EVELYN CHAZONOFF BEAUCHEMIN	Jill Frappier
HENRY MARKOWITZ	Alex Poch-Goldin
LYNN CHARNEY	Janet-Laine Green
PHIL KOBLIN	Chuck Shamata
RABBI RON MADOFF	Paul Soles
FRANCES LEITMAN	Victoria Mitchell
Producer	James Roy
Recording Engineer	John McCarthy
Special Effects	Matt Willcott
	Wayne Richards
Associate Producer	Sandra Broitman
	Colleen Woods
Script Editor	Dave Carley

Past Imperfect

Scene One: Beauchemins' house

[*Sound: (off) running tap water; Evelyn splashing her face. Continues under:*
Sound: Phone ringing.]

MICHEL	Hello?
MAROWITZ	*(Filtered)* Michel Beauchemin?
MICHEL	Yes.
MAROWITZ	The Michel Beauchemin who is about to be honoured with the Berman Medal —
MICHEL	Who is this?
MAROWITZ	— in recognition of his "life-long commitment to human rights"?
MICHEL	*(Edgy)* Who's speaking?
EVELYN	*(Off)* Michel? Who is it?
MICHEL	Do I know you?
MAROWITZ	This is your past calling. This is your past, catching up with you.
MICHEL	What are you talking about?
EVELYN	*(Off)* Michel?
MAROWITZ	Farber.
EVELYN	*(Off)* Michel?
MAROWITZ	Aaron Farber.

[*Sound: (off) Evelyn turns tap off. Stands in bathroom doorway.*]

EVELYN	*(Loud whisper)* Who are you talking to?
MAROWITZ	You remember Aaron Farber.
MICHEL	*(To Evelyn)* An acquaintance.
EVELYN	At this hour?
MAROWITZ	I know what you did. *(Beat)* I know where you were.
MICHEL	Yes.
MAROWITZ	Hell will freeze over before you get the Berman Medal.
MICHEL	*(Bluffing)* Thank you.
MAROWITZ	Good evening, Monsieur Beauchemin.
	[*Sound: Marowitz hangs up. A moment's pause, then Michel hangs up.*]
EVELYN	They couldn't have waited 'til tomorrow morning?
MICHEL	*(Faking it)* He's new. You know what they're like, the young ones.
EVELYN	You were never like that when you were young.
MICHEL	The rules have changed.
EVELYN	How did he know you weren't sleeping?
MICHEL	I'll see he doesn't do it again.

Past Imperfect

Scene Two: *Canadian Jewish Council*

[*Sound: The click of a button, the whir of a slide projector. Continues under:*]

PHIL

This is a nice one. I think this is Africa. (Beat) Is this Africa?

LYNN

It's too early to quiz me.

PHIL

The ceremony's in less than a week. We've got to plough through five hundred slides. Then we argue over which fifty we like best. *(Beat)* Drink your coffee.

LYNN

I thought being president meant I'd never have to do this kind of work.

PHIL

Being president means having final approval. *(Beat)* What did he do in Africa?

LYNN

River blindness.

PHIL

River blindness is good. And it's a good picture. Beauchemin looks ever-so-modest. The kids look ever-so-grateful. They'll love it.

LYNN

It's too early for cynicism.

PHIL

Me? A cynic?

LYNN

He's done some terrific work. (Beat) Can I tell you a secret?

PHIL

Yes.

LYNN

Promise not to tell?

PHIL

No.

LYNN

When I was a kid, I wanted to be a Michel Beauchemin when I grew up.

PHIL   You wouldn't look good in a moustache.

LYNN   I'm serious. He was Albert Schweitzer and Raoul Wallenberg and Gregory Peck all rolled into one.

PHIL   Gregory Peck?

LYNN   *To Kill a Mockingbird. (Beat)* Such dignity.

PHIL   Gregory Peck isn't getting the medal. Next slide.

            [*Sound: Click of button, whir of slide machine.*]

LYNN   Where's this?

PHIL   If I'm not mistaken, this is deep in the jungles of Ottawa.

LYNN   Ottawa?

PHIL   A book drive. They collect used books, then send them overseas. To help boost literacy rates. That kind of thing.

LYNN   Boring.

PHIL   Literacy is *not* boring.

LYNN   The slide. It's boring. We're not going to stage a black tie ceremony and show a picture of Beauchemin holding a box of books. It's not...

PHIL   Sexy?

LYNN   Flattering. We want to flatter the man. *(Beat)* He deserves to be flattered.

Scene Three: Beauchemins' house

[*Sound: Breakfast backdrop: morning radio show, toaster popping.*
Sound: Knife spreading butter on toast.]

EVELYN   *(Approaching)* The acquaintance who called last night, what did he tell you?

[*Sound: Plates placed on table, coffee poured*]

MICHEL   He's not an acquaintance. Strictly speaking.

EVELYN   A colleague?

MICHEL   I told you. He's...he's new at External Affairs. Wet behind the ears. You know what they're like. So eager. So many questions.

EVELYN   *(Concerned)* What did he ask you?

MICHEL   I won't bore you with the dry details. Pass the marmalade, please.

EVELYN   You were up all night.

MICHEL   Did you buy this at the market? The marmalade?

EVELYN   He said something. Something that bothered you. You didn't stop tossing and turning. I could practically hear your anxiety every time you breathed. *(Beat)* What's troubling you, Michel?

MICHEL   *(Pause)* You really want to know.

EVELYN   I really want to know.

MICHEL   My speech. For the Berman Medal. I have only three days to finish it. I have finished it. But it feels...incomplete. I've started to rewrite it. In my head. That's what I was doing last night, in bed. Rewriting my speech. That's what I have to do today. I have to collect all the changes that have been swimming in my head and put them down on paper. I want the speech to be just right. To be perfect. *(Beat)* It's an important award, you know.

EVELYN   *(Proudly)* I know.

MICHEL   I have to strike the right note.

[*Sound: Evelyn kisses Michel's hand.*]

EVELYN   Sweetheart, don't worry. It's —

MICHEL   It's only one of the most important honours a diplomat could hope for.

EVELYN   You have a shelf full of awards. A wall full of pictures. Michel shaking hands with the President. Michel standing next to the Pope. There'll be more to come, I assure you. More prizes. More pictures. This is one more feather in the distinguished cap of Michel Beauchemin.

MICHEL   It's a big feather.

EVELYN   You looked exhausted, sweetheart. Why don't you go back to bed and get some sleep?

MICHEL   No. I have a speech to write. To rewrite. *(Beat)* A speech to perfect.

Scene Four: Canadian Jewish Council

[*Sound: The click of a button, the whir of a slide projector. Continues under:*]

LYNN   I like that one.

PHIL   I don't know. Beauchemin on a teeter-totter?

LYNN — Look at the kid's face. You can eat it up. *(Beat)* Where was this one taken?

PHIL — Israel.

LYNN — I thought so.

PHIL — Playgrounds for Peace. And they shall beat their swords into swings. That kind of thing. Another attempt at promoting peace between Arabs and Israelis.

LYNN — Let's end with it. It's a nice way to wrap up the show.

[*Sound: Phone ringing. Button clicked.*]

LYNN — Yes?

RECEPTION — *(Speaker phone)* Henry Marowitz to see you.

LYNN — Oh, God.

PHIL — Tell him we're busy.

REC — He says it's urgent.

LYNN — Henry thinks everything is urgent. *(Beat)* Send him in. *(To Phil)* The last thing I need is Henry foaming at the mouth.

PHIL — His bark is worse than his bite.

LYNN — I don't like his bark.

[*Sound: Door opens, closes.*]

LYNN & PHIL { — Henry...

MAROWITZ — Phil. Lynn. Am I interrupting some —

PHIL   Yes.

MAROWITZ   This is worth an interruption. *(Beat)* Ah, will you look at that. This year's Berman Medal winner, sitting pretty on a see-saw. It's enough to make you weep.

LYNN   What can we do for you, Henry?

MAROWITZ   Me? I don't want anything. But the Canadian Jewish Council can do itself a big favour and forget about the medal. Cancel the ceremony. Do whatever you have to do, but don't let Michel Beauchemin near you. Or your hands will be stained with blood, too.

PHIL   Stained with blood?

MAROWITZ   Jewish blood.

LYNN   Of course.

MAROWITZ   The blood of Aaron Farber.

LYNN   Who?

MAROWITZ   Tell me, Phil. How did someone with such an appalling ignorance of history end up council president?

PHIL   It's called an election.

LYNN   If you came here to insult —

MAROWITZ   I came here to illuminate.

LYNN   Well then illuminate.

MAROWITZ   As you know, I'm organizing a new exhibition at the institute.

102

LYNN   I didn't know.

MAROWITZ   Well, you should. It's sponsored by the Gilman Foundation.

PHIL   Congratulations.

MAROWITZ   The Face of Fascism: Quebec in the 30s and 40s.

LYNN   Fascism?

PHIL   Interesting title.

LYNN   More inflammatory than interesting, but we've come to expect as much from Henry.

MAROWITZ   Nineteen thirty-three, *Le Devoir*. "When Hitler attacks the Jew, he attacks the most formidable power of deceit in the world because the Jews not only control the newspapers in all the important cities in the world, but also many press agencies which are like the arteries of information." Nineteen thirty-four. Interns at five French Montreal hospitals stage a strike when a Jewish colleague is hired. Nineteen thirty-five, *Le Devoir*. "Jews seem to dominate certain Montreal neighbourhoods. If the truth be told, their apparent dominance is due more to the brazen criminality of a minority than to the size of their population."

LYNN   You and Mordecai Richler, both. Quebec didn't have a monopoly on anti-Semitism, Henry.

PHIL   What does this have to do with Beauchemin?

MAROWITZ   You want a picture for your slide show? Try this one on for size. I found it doing research at *The Gazette* for the exhibition. Dug it up in the archives. Not your average crowd scene.

               [*A brief pause as Lynn and Phil ponder the photograph.*]

103

LYNN   What does this have to do with Beauchemin?

MAROWITZ   Look at the left side of the picture. Bottom corner. Third man in.

PHIL   Beauchemin?

MAROWITZ   Beauchemin.

LYNN   Where was this taken?

MAROWITZ   Montreal. Nineteen-thirty nine. A group of right-wing extremists take to the streets. Saint Lawrence Boulevard, to be precise. They start tossing stones at Jewish shops. Aaron Farber, 64, steps out of his tailor shop and tries to plead with the crowd. He's attacked. That's Farber in the middle of the picture. The bloody lump on the ground. A…stone's throw away from Beauchemin. The next day Farber dies in hospital. Almost sixty years later, Michel Beauchemin is given a medal honouring his life's work.

LYNN   I knew about the incident. I didn't know his name was Farber.

PHIL   Does Beauchemin know?

MAROWITZ   Of course he knows. He was there.

PHIL   The picture. Does he know about the picture?

MAROWITZ   I sent it by courier first thing this morning. It should be in his blood-stained hands by now. So, are you going to write the press release, or shall I?

LYNN   This is the council's concern, Henry. Not yours.

MAROWITZ   Wrongo, Mrs. President. There is not a chance in hell you are giving a medal to that Nazi.

104

LYNN   Thank you for bringing the matter to our
              attention, Henry.

MAROWITZ   You're not gonna let her railroad you, are you
              Phil?

LYNN   Phil was just about to see you to the door.
              Weren't you, Phil? *(Beat)* Phil?

PHIL   *(Pause)* Yes. *(Beat)* Yes, I was.

Scene Five: Beauchemin's study

[*Sound: Beauchemin tapping computer keyboard.
Continues under:*]

MICHEL   *(Internal)* The ideals which Isaac Berman
              pursued throughout his lifetime should be
              inscribed in stone and used as a foundation
              upon which all our lives are built. Past winners
              of the Berman Medal have inspired human
              rights workers around the world. The Medal has
              become a synonym for the fundamental rights
              each of us is entitled to. I am deeply honoured,
              and greatly humbled, by —

              [*Sound/biz: (off) doorbell rings. Evelyn answers.
              We hear bits of her brief conversation, but not the
              details. The door closes. We can hear Evelyn tear
              open a large envelope.*]

MICHEL   Evelyn? Who was that? *(Pause)* Evelyn?

Scene Six: Canadian Jewish Council

[*Sound: Whir of slide projector.*]

LYNN   Shut that damn thing off.

[*Sound: Click of button as projector is turned off and begins to cool down.*]

LYNN   His wife is Jewish, you know. Evelyn Chazonoff. Evelyn Chazonoff Beauchemin. She grew up in an Orthodox home.

PHIL   His second wife. She's his second wife.

LYNN   So what? He's been married to her for a long time. Anti-semites don't usually make it a habit of marrying Jews.

PHIL   You don't think he's anti-Semitic?

LYNN   I don't know what to think.

PHIL   This isn't a picture I'd like to keep on my mantelpiece.

LYNN   It makes no sense.

PHIL   The way Marowitz describes it —

LYNN   Marowitz wasn't there.

PHIL   Beauchemin was.

LYNN   *(Almost to herself)* What happened?

PHIL   Aaron Farber was killed.

LYNN   The pieces, they just don't fit.

PHIL   According to Henry —

LYNN   Henry Marowitz is a virulent anti anti-Semite.

PHIL   *(Beat)* A *what*?

LYNN   He hates anti-Semites.

PHIL   As opposed to — what? — inviting them over
              for tea?

LYNN   The faintest whiff of anti-Semitism sends him
              into hysterics.

PHIL   Stoning a man to death is not what I'd call a
              faint whiff.

LYNN   We have to proceed cautiously. Beauchemin is a
              very public figure. Marowitz will have you
              believe that the Jews of Montreal were being
              mowed down on the streets, and that
              Beauchemin was leading the mob. What
              happened to Farber was...was —

PHIL   Unforgivable.

              [*The word hangs in the air.*]

              Scene Seven: Beauchemin's study

MICHEL   What's wrong? You look...Who was that? At
              the door?

EVELYN   Do you know Henry Marowitz?

MICHEL   Vaguely.

EVELYN   He sent us a package. A letter, addressed to you
              and me. And a photograph. *(Pause)* Do you
              recognize it?

              [*A long, disquieting silence.*]

EVELYN   Do you recognize it?

MICHEL   *(Pause)* Yes.

EVELYN   That's all you have to say?

107

MICHEL   It isn't me.

EVELYN   That's not you?

MICHEL   It's a different me.

EVELYN   It's you.

MICHEL   It's who I was. I was young, very young. Nineteen, maybe twenty. It was a long time ago. Before you knew me. *(Beat)* Before I knew myself.

           [*Another moment of silence.*]

MICHEL   Say something.

EVELYN   *(Pause)* I'm not sure what's worse. That you were there. Or that you never told me you were.

           [*Sound: Footsteps as Evelyn begins to walk away.*]

MICHEL   Where are you going?

EVELYN   *(Off)* I need some water. *(Beat)* I feel faint.

           Scene Eight: Beauchemins' Kitchen

           [*Sound: Water being poured into glass filled with ice.*]

MICHEL   *(Approaching)* You have to understand.

           [*Sound: Michel easing into a chair.*]

EVELYN   Yes. Please. Make me understand.

MICHEL   I can't. It's not something I...

EVELYN   All this time you knew and you said nothing.

MICHEL   It was so long ago.

EVELYN   Stop saying that!

              [*Sound: Evelyn bangs her glass of water down on
              the table.*]

MICHEL   I'll get a dishtowel.

              [*Sound: Michel rising out of his chair.*]

EVELYN   Sit down!

              [*Evelyn's tone surprises her. She lowers her voice a
              few notches.*]

EVELYN   Sit down.

              [*Sound: Michel returns to his seat. He waits a
              while before puncturing the silence.*]

MICHEL   You have never been in a crowd.

EVELYN   I've been in a crowd.

MICHEL   I don't mean a busy mall or a crowded street. I
              mean a *real* crowd. A crowd that is so...so alive,
              it takes on a life of its own. *(Pause)* I can see you
              don't know what I mean. It's difficult to explain.

EVELYN   It's what you owe me, at the very least. An
              explanation.

MICHEL   It only happened to me once. A crowd like that.
              A mob.

EVELYN   Only once.

MICHEL   It overtakes you. It...it swallows you up. You are
              not you anymore. You are part of something
              much bigger than you.

EVELYN   "I was only following orders."

MICHEL   I was so young. So, so ripe. *(Beat)* One person stomps his feet. Then another. Then another. Soon everyone is stomping their feet. Stomp. Stomp. Stomp. It sounds like thunder. A roar. A river.

EVELYN   *(Drily)* A river.

MICHEL   A raging river. You can't stop it. You..you are swept up. Swept away. Into a sea.

EVELYN   A sea.

MICHEL   A sea of arms. A sea of eyes. You are part of it. You feel powerful. Invincible.

EVELYN   And Aaron Farber? How did he feel?

MICHEL   *(Pause)* I never hit him.

EVELYN   "I didn't pull the trigger."

MICHEL   I had some stones in my hand, it's true. I threw a few. But not at him. I am sure. *(Pause)* I threw them... *(Beat)* Where they landed, I can't remember.

EVELYN   *(Drily)* It was so long ago.

MICHEL   Yes.

Scene Nine: Canadian Jewish Council

[*Sound: Nervous tapping of a pen on a table.*]

PHIL   Are you gonna tap like that all morning or will you start taking requests?

LYNN   I'm trying to decide what to do.

PHIL   You're the prez.

LYNN   You always say that.

PHIL   It's the truth.

LYNN   I think we should call him in. Before we rush to any judgement. Before we do anything else. He should have the opportunity to... explain himself.

PHIL   He's gonna have a lot of explaining to do.

LYNN   Let's hear what he has to say.

PHIL   I'm looking forward to it.

LYNN   You sound like Marowitz.

PHIL   *(Pause: the penny drops)* Wait. Waitwaitwaitwait.

LYNN   What?

PHIL   Now I get it.

LYNN   Get what?

PHIL   Why you've been jumping hoops trying to justify -

LYNN   I am not trying —

PHIL   You nominated him. You submitted his nomination for the Berman Medal.

LYNN   Everyone endorsed my nomination. Including you.

PHIL   You have more at stake.

LYNN   This isn't about stakes.

PHIL   How's it gonna look when it comes out that our

president threw a party for a war criminal?

LYNN   War criminal?

PHIL   I'm just imagining the tabloid headlines. And believe me, heads are going to roll.

LYNN   Is this all you care about? Headlines?

PHIL   I don't want to be seen near this man.

LYNN   You don't have much choice. We'll ask him in this afternoon. You can stand in the closet if you like.

Scene Ten: Beauchemins' Bedroom

[*Sound: Rattle of hangers as clothes are pulled out of closet. Drawers opened and closed. Evelyn is fuelled by a smouldering energy. Continues under:*]

MICHEL   What are you doing?

EVELYN   I'm leaving.

MICHEL   You're leaving me?

EVELYN   I didn't say I was leaving you. I said I was leaving.

MICHEL   I see. *(Beat)* Where are you going?

EVELYN   To Frances.

MICHEL   Frances. *(Beat)* For how long?

EVELYN   I don't know.

MICHEL   You don't know.

EVELYN   I need some time alone.

MICHEL   You won't be alone. Frances will be there.

EVELYN   I need some time away. From you. I feel so...so —

MICHEL   This is your solution? Running away?

EVELYN   I am not "running away." I have to have some
                distance from —

MICHEL   I'm not contagious.

EVELYN   I didn't say you were.

MICHEL   You talk like I have a disease.

EVELYN   Don't put words in my mouth.

MICHEL   I never threw another stone. Never.

                [*Sound: Evelyn zips up her bag.*]

EVELYN   You never told me.

MICHEL   I have always told you the truth.

EVELYN   Not the whole truth.

MICHEL   I have never lied to you.

EVELYN   You hid your past from me. You were afraid I
                would —

MICHEL   You would have misunderstood.

EVELYN   You had no right to assume what I would or
                would not have done.

MICHEL   And if I told you? You wouldn't have married me?

EVELYN   I would have married a different you.

113

MICHEL	I am the same me. The Michel you married and the Michel who threw stones, they are two different Michels.
EVELYN	There is a third Michel. The one who keeps dark secrets to himself. The one who didn't trust his wife with the truth.
MICHEL	I didn't think it mattered.
EVELYN	*(Walking off)* That's for me to decide.
MICHEL	You're being impulsive. *(Beat)* Evelyn. *(Beat)* Evelyn!

Scene Eleven: Beauchemin's study

[*Sound: Beauchemin tapping computer keyboard. Continues under:*]

MICHEL	*(Internal)* I would like to take a few moments to address our youth. If we are to sow the seeds for a better world tomorrow, we must place those seeds in the hands of those who will live to see the fruits of their labours. We are quick to dismiss our young people as irresponsible. Disrespectful. Even defiant. We must recognize their wayward, rebellious ways as merely a rite of passage. A healthy transition. We all know of the long-haired hippies who were handcuffed at riots in the sixties who are now clean-shaven captains of industry. The young girl with green hair and an earring in her lip who curses a blue streak, she may be prime minister one day. To be an angry teenager is to follow life's script. They fill me with hope, these young people. They remind me that change is not only possible, it is inevitable. There are a few holdouts, a few men and women who will never conform, but they are the —

[*Sound: Ringing phone. Michel picks up receiver.*]

MICHEL   *(Hint of smugness)* You changed your mind.

LYNN   *(Filtered)* Monsieur Beauchemin?

MICHEL   I'm sorry. I thought you were —

LYNN   This is Lynn Charney. From the Canadian Jewish Council.

MICHEL   Oh, yes. Of course. How are you?

LYNN   I'm fine. I'm sorry to call you on such short notice, but we were wondering, if it's not inconvenient, if you could drop by our offices later today.

MICHEL   What for?

LYNN   There are a few items we'd like to go over with you.

MICHEL   Items?

LYNN   For the ceremony.

MICHEL   Can we not discuss them over the phone?

LYNN   It really would be best if you came in.

MICHEL   Today?

LYNN   Yes.

MICHEL   When?

LYNN   Two o'clock. Is two o'clock okay?

MICHEL   *(Pause)* Yes.

Making Waves

Scene Twelve: Frances' Den

[*Sound: Drawers being opened and shut, hangers clattering as Evelyn unpacks.*]

FRANCES   You can stay as long as you like.

EVELYN   It won't be forever. Just until...

FRANCES   Until?

EVELYN   I don't know. Until I understand all this.

FRANCES   That could take a while. You've been hit by a bomb.

EVELYN   Bombs are usually dropped by the enemy.

FRANCES   He didn't actually kill him, right?

EVELYN   What's the difference? He was right there. Right in the thick of it. If he...If he had told me. If he had come clean when we first met, we could have... *(Pause)* On my way over here, I had this...this terrible thought. It's ridiculous, really.

FRANCES   *(Waiting)* Well...

EVELYN   What if...What if he married me to, to atone for what he did.

FRANCES   Evelyn...

EVELYN   Maybe marrying me was his way of washing away his guilt.

FRANCES   You're right. *(Beat)* It's ridiculous.

EVELYN   I know. *(Beat)* Then I started feeling guilty for having these guilty thoughts about Michel's guilt.

FRANCES   *(Gentle teasing)* Oy! So much guilt.

EVELYN   There's more. More guilt. I started wondering if I was being punished for marrying out of the faith.

FRANCES   Why're you doing this to yourself?

EVELYN   The fact is, this wouldn't have happened if he was Jewish.

FRANCES   The fact is, you love him. Don't rewrite the past.

EVELYN   It's the future I'm worried about. I can't go back to what was. I can't. Our life together has been a lie.

FRANCES   You're not being fair.

EVELYN   You don't know what it's like. I feel like I'm in mourning.

FRANCES   Who died?

EVELYN   Aaron Farber. *(Beat)* Me. Part of me. Me and Michel. *(Beat)* One phone call and a marriage unravels.

FRANCES   Now what? How do you...reravel an unravelled marriage?

EVELYN   Reravel?

FRANCES   I don't know. I just made it up. I'm new to all this.

EVELYN   So am I. It's all so new. So strange. So very —

FRANCES   You're shivering. You need a drink.

EVELYN   Scotch. On the rocks.

FRANCES   Scotch? Since when?

EVELYN   Since rarely.

FRANCES   And this is a rarely.

EVELYN   Very.

Scene Thirteen: Canadian Jewish Council

MICHEL   Henry Marowitz gave you this photograph.

LYNN   Yes.

MICHEL   Where did he get it?

PHIL   With all due respect, Monsieur Beauchemin, we're less concerned with who took the photograph than who is in it.

LYNN   You can appreciate how we're in a very difficult situation. The ceremony is this Saturday. That leaves us very little time to explain to people how...I don't have to tell you how highly regarded you are. That's not the issue. Your work for peace in the Middle East. Your commitment to —

PHIL   The problem is that the Berman Medal is not a Boy Scout badge. There's a lot riding on this award. A lot more than a flattering picture in Monday's paper.

LYNN   *(Annoyed)* What Phil is trying to say —

PHIL   What I'm saying is that people are going to have one helluva time trying to match Michel-Beauchemin-the-human-rights-hero with Michel-Beauchemin-the-the...

MICHEL   The stone thrower. I have not thrown a stone in over fifty years.

PHIL   Congratulations.

MICHEL   I did not come here today to apologize.

LYNN   "Explanation" might be a more appropriate word.

PHIL   I like "apology."

MICHEL   I will not apologize for what I was, briefly, once upon a time. Nor will I sit here and justify my record as a public servant.

LYNN   Your record speaks for itself. That's not the —

MICHEL   My concern is that my past will be misunderstood. Misconstrued. I cannot justify what happened. Nor can I fully explain it. There is no easy explanation. I can only point to what I have done since then. You must judge for yourself.

LYNN   It is not for us to judge. Not entirely. We're accountable to the board.

MICHEL   Then you must speak to the board.

PHIL   Oh, we will. Trust us.

Scene Fourteen: Beauchemin's office

[*Sound: Ringing phone. Receiver picked up.*]

MAROWITZ   *(Filtered)* Marowitz. *(Beat)* Hello?...Hello?

MICHEL   Your victory is hollow.

MAROWITZ   Who is this?

MICHEL   I won't get the medal. Thanks to you.

MAROWITZ	Well, if it isn't the little storm trooper himself.
MICHEL	You could not let bygones be bygones.
MAROWITZ	Aaron Farber is not a "bygone."
MICHEL	This has nothing to do with Aaron Farber. All you see is a Jew.
MAROWITZ	A Jew who was stoned to death.
MICHEL	You have divided the world into two: Jews, and everyone else.
MAROWITZ	Spare me the geography lesson.
MICHEL	Everywhere you turn, you see a hatred for Jews.
MAROWITZ	You don't have to look far.
MICHEL	Hatred breeds hostility.
MAROWITZ	You would know.
MICHEL	I have known hatred. First-hand. It is behind me. You insist on throwing it back at me.
MAROWITZ	You're the one who did the throwing. Now you have to face the music.
MICHEL	Who are you to judge me? To judge my life?
MAROWITZ	Who are you to decide you've paid for what you did?
MICHEL	How much must I pay for my past?
MAROWITZ	I don't know. I'll tell you this much the price of the Berman Medal is out of your reach.
MICHEL	*(Pause)* So. You got what you wanted.

MAROWITZ   No. You got what you deserved.

Scene Fifteen: Canadian Jewish Council

PHIL   He's unrepentant.

LYNN   He's defensive.

PHIL   Whose side are you on?

LYNN   It's not a question of sides. I'm trying very hard to make sense of all this. We need to look at the whole picture. We'll call an emergency meeting. First thing tomorrow morning.

PHIL   We're wasting our time, dragging in the board to discuss something that isn't worth discussing. The man we were about to honour is guilty. Guilty as sin. He was a rabid nationalist who stoned a defenceless Jewish shopkeeper to death. There's nothing to discuss.

LYNN   I am not condoning what happened. But I'm not sure it's an open and shut case. That's why we'll meet tomorrow.

PHIL   And what are you going to say when everyone's gathered round the conference table?

LYNN   Why me? Why not both of us?

PHIL   You're the pres —

LYNN   Don't! Don't say it.

PHIL   Why do you get so riled when I —

LYNN   It's not what you say. It's how you say it.

PHIL   I see. You don't like the way I talk.

LYNN   I don't like your attitude.

PHIL   Well then, why don't you bring it up at the board meeting. Michel Beauchemin's bloody past. Phil Koblin's bad attitude.

LYNN   You can't get over that I won and you didn't. You think you'd make a much better president.

PHIL   I would have a different approach.

LYNN   You hate that a woman is running the show.

PHIL   I would have a different approach.

LYNN   Well, as long as I'm president, as you love to remind me, we'll be taking my approach. The issue calls for a rational discussion. That's how we'll proceed. Rationally.

PHIL   I'm glad I'm not in your shoes.

LYNN   On the contrary. You can't stand the fact that you're not.

Scene Sixteen: Frances's backyard

[*Sound: Logs being split with an axe. Continues under:*]

FRANCES   *(Grunting)* This is what I do when I have to work things out. *(Beat)* It's cheaper than a therapist, and more productive.

EVELYN   You burn all these logs?

FRANCES   Most of 'em. Sometimes I have more than I need. If I've gone through a crisis. You wanna know the state of my mental health? Look at my log pile. *(Beat)* Here. Have a go.

EVELYN   I'm no lumberjack.

FRANCES   Neither am I. Go on. You could use a few good whacks.

[*Sound: Evelyn has a go, misses the log and hits the stump on which it stands. Both women laugh.*]

FRANCES   Try again.

[*Sound: Evelyn tries again...and splits the log in half. We can hear her exhilaration, a sense of release.*]

FRANCES   Bravo! Care for another?

EVELYN   *(Still catching her breath)* Sure.

[*Sound: Evelyn has another satisfying crack at another log. Beneath the women's laughter we hear faint applause, which becomes louder as their laughter fades.*]

MICHEL   *(Off)* You're a real Paul Bunyan.

FRANCES   *(Pointedly)* Or Lizzie Borden.

MICHEL   *(Off)* Am I interrupting?

FRANCES   I was just leaving.

EVELYN   Frances...

FRANCES   I have some things to do inside. *(Beat)* I *do*.

[*Sound: Evelyn chops another log. In her grunts and groans we hear more anger than exhilaration.*]

MICHEL   I understand how you feel.

EVELYN   No. *(Beat)* No. *(Beat)* You're the one who keeps saying I won't understand what you did. Why you did it. Why you kept it from me. But when it comes to me, what I'm going through, well,

then, you understand all too well. Is that it? You
can understand me but I can't understand you?
(Beat) No thanks.

[*Sound: Another log split.*]

MICHEL   When are you coming home?

EVELYN   When you start explaining I'll consider
coming home.

MICHEL   It's not that easy.

EVELYN   I didn't say it was.

MICHEL   You're asking me to open a box I've kept shut
for almost sixty years.

EVELYN   Yes.

MICHEL   And if I can't? You'll never return?

EVELYN   Don't! *(Beat)* Don't twist things around. Don't
make me into the bad guy. Don't blame it all on
me. Or Marowitz. Or anyone else. This is your
responsibility. You do what has to be done.

[*Sound: Evelyn splits another log.*]

MICHEL   You've been drinking. I can smell it.

EVELYN   *(Laughing)* Let's play a game, shall we? Let's play
"Discredit Evelyn". Let's pretend she's too drunk
to know what she's saying. *(Changes tone)* I'm
not drunk. I know exactly what I'm saying.

MICHEL   You're being swept away by your emotions.

EVELYN   Don't make the mistake of not taking me
seriously.

124

MICHEL   I'm taking you home. You need to rest.

EVELYN   I will not live in a house filled with half-truths and white lies. Do you understand me? *(Beat)* Do you?!

MICHEL   Yes.

EVELYN   Goodbye, Michel.

MICHEL   Where are you going?

EVELYN   I'm not going anywhere. You are.

                [*Sound: Another log is split.*]

Scene Seventeen: Rabbi's office

                [*Sound: Cantorial music. Continues under: Sound: Knock on door.*]

RABBI MADOFF   Come in.

                [*Sound: Door opens, Michel steps in.*]

RABBI   My dear Michel.

MICHEL   *(Off)* Rabbi.

                [*Sound: Michel closes door behind him.*]

RABBI   Come in, come in. I was just listening to Jan Peerce. *The Art of the Cantor.* Exquisite.

                [*Sound: Madoff lowers volume on tape deck and begins rifling through some loose papers.*]

RABBI   I received a fax today. From Henry Marowitz.

MICHEL   Oh, Christ!

RABBI   Not my first words, but an understandable choice.

MICHEL	The man is a snake.
RABBI	Many in the community are willing to forgive Henry his attitude in light of his steadfast devotion to exposing wrongs.
MICHEL	He's a pit bull.
RABBI	A snake. A pit bull. You're working your way right through the ark.
MICHEL	I wanted to tell you first hand.
RABBI	Henry beat you to the punch.
MICHEL	Have you seen the photograph?
RABBI	No.
MICHEL	You will. It's just a matter of time before it's on the front page.
RABBI	You think so?
MICHEL	I am sure of it.
RABBI	And how does that make you feel?
MICHEL	*(Pause)* Angry.
RABBI	Angry. How so?
MICHEL	*(Pause)* Rabbi, you've known me since I married Evelyn. Am I hateful man?
RABBI	No.
MICHEL	Bloodthirsty?
RABBI	Of course not.
MICHEL	Am I a killer?

RABBI	Michel...
MICHEL	I did not kill Aaron Farber. That's what people will think. That I pelted Aaron Farber with stones until he died.
RABBI	Does that concern you? What other people think?
MICHEL	I have devoted my life to mending the world. *Tikkun Olam.* You taught me that phrase.
RABBI	It was not mine to give. I merely passed it on to you.
MICHEL	To have a life's work undone by a photograph.
RABBI	A man was killed, Michel.
MICHEL	*(Angrily)* I know that! I was there! *(Pause. Lowers his voice)* I'm sorry.
RABBI	We live in a world where we may forever lose the colour grey. Everything is either black or white. Good or bad. Right or wrong. Everyone wants quick answers. Easy solutions. No one can be bothered with the subtle shades, the grey, murky areas where there are no absolutes.
MICHEL	Are you saying you forgive me?
RABBI	Is that why you came? To seek my forgiveness?
MICHEL	No.
RABBI	It is not for me to grant it. You are in a difficult position, Michel. You have a high public profile, and a private life to nurture. The public might not be nearly as forgiving as Evelyn.
MICHEL	She's left me.

127

RABBI   Evelyn?

MICHEL   Temporarily. I'm sure.

RABBI   You don't sound certain. *(Beat)* You fear you might lose her.

MICHEL   Yes.

RABBI   It can't be easy for her. In front of her is the man she loves. Behind her is her people, and a history marked by anti-Semitism, deadly and otherwise. Who can blame her for not knowing which way to turn.

MICHEL   She thinks I lied. I never lied. *(Pause)* I never told anyone. I didn't think anyone had to know because of all the work I have done since then.

RABBI   You owed it to Evelyn.

MICHEL   I was afraid she wouldn't understand.

RABBI   Now you are afraid you may lose her. Which is worse?

[*We can hear Michel's response in his silence.*]

RABBI   Why didn't you tell her?

MICHEL   You think it's easy.

RABBI   I never suggested it was.

MICHEL   We do things, all of us, that we keep close to our hearts. Things we are not proud of. An ugly thought. A thoughtless deed. We put them in little boxes, these, these sins, and we store them beside our hearts. We leave them there for a long time. So long, you forget they are there. By the time you are my age, you have a thousand little boxes.

RABBI

That makes for a heavy heart.

MICHEL

The boxes from long ago, they're covered with dust. It's easier to leave them untouched.

RABBI

You may have a thousand little boxes, Michel, but only one has Aaron Farber's name on it.

MICHEL

What are you saying?

RABBI

I strongly suggest you start dusting.

Scene Eighteen: Canadian Jewish Council

[*Sound: Door slamming shut as Lynn enters boardroom. She bangs her briefcase down on the conference table.*]

LYNN

You little shit.

PHIL

Good morning.

LYNN

You had no right. No right. It's immoral. It's appalling. It's disgusting. Not to mention uncon —

PHIL

Now, now. Let's not lose perspective. I cancelled a board meeting. It's not like I diddled some kid in a school yard.

LYNN

I *know* what you did. Kornish called me this morning.

PHIL

Kornish. He's a piece of work, that one. He wondered if we could delay the ceremony. Like, hello? Eight other board members agreed with me.

LYNN

Not quite. Not according to Kornish. He told me all about your conference call last night. Your very impassioned, very superficial account of what happened. You stacked the cards, then took a vote. It's unconstitutional, let alone unethical. It's deceitful.

PHIL   It's a fait accompli. Giving Beauchemin the Berman is a non-starter. It's a "no go." Not now. Not ever. Not in a million years.

LYNN   The man is entitled to a fair hearing.

PHIL   He's entitled to dick.

LYNN   You are pathetic.

PHIL   If you don't have the balls to do the right thing, that's your problem, not mine.

LYNN   Is that what you told the board during your private little poll? That poor little Lynn doesn't have any backbone? That maybe Phil should be president?

PHIL   They'll draw their own conclusions.

LYNN   You won't get away with this. I won't let you. To begin with, you were in no position to make a decision based on a "poll." There are things called by-laws.

PHIL   You sound just like Freitag. He also got his knickers in a knot over the con-sti-tu-tion. So I asked the other board members point-blank, "What's a by-law compared to a human life?"

LYNN   You are disgusting. You're using Aaron Farber as a pawn. You're exploiting his death to help stage your coup.

PHIL   A coup, is it? Is that what I've been doing?

LYNN   You'll do whatever it takes to throw me out of office so you can call the shots. Even if it means dancing on Aaron Farber's grave.

PHIL   I didn't send Aaron Farber to his grave.

LYNN   Do you think I'm blind to what Beauchemin did? You think I'm indifferent to what happened to Farber? I felt sick when Marowitz showed us the picture. I couldn't believe it. I kept comparing Beauchemin in the picture to the Beauchemin that we all know. The UNICEF work, the boat people, the child labourers.

PHIL   We're all familiar with his good works. I can show you some slides.

LYNN   I kept thinking. "How is it possible? How is it possible that the same person who once stoned a man could one day be front-and-centre in the human rights movement?" That's all I could think of last night. And then it clicked. The pieces fell into place. Beauchemin is the perfect recipient for the Berman. Only someone once filled with so much hate can give us that much hope.

PHIL   Hope?

LYNN   Yes. Look at what Beauchemin once did.

PHIL   *(Drily)* I've looked.

LYNN   Look at what he's become. If that isn't cause for hope, I don't know what is.

PHIL   I see. You're suggesting that Michel Beauchemin become a poster boy for "hope."

LYNN   By giving him the medal we'd give him the chance to show that people can change. He's living proof. He's made a hundred and eighty degree turn. He's redeemed himself.

PHIL	The Berman medal isn't about redemption.
LYNN	We'd be saying, "Listen to this man's story. Be inspired by it."
PHIL	I'm sure Aaron Farber would be moved to tears.
LYNN	You don't get it, do you?
PHIL	I get it. Let's forget about the past. Let's —
LYNN	No. Don't just remember the past. Learn from it.
PHIL	Michel Beauchemin is in no position to give anyone any history lessons. And neither are you. You've lost a lot of credibility over this, Lynn. It's too bad. Some people — I won't mention names — may soon be calling for your resignation.
LYNN	No way. I'll fight you over this one. It's a matter of principle.
PHIL	Principles have nothing to do with it. You know that. It's all politics.
LYNN	*(Pause)* You really don't deserve to be here.
PHIL	Take it up at the next board meeting.

Scene Nineteen: Beauchemin's living room

[Sound: Roaring fire in fireplace. Continues under:
Sound: (off) doorbell.
Sound: (off) Michel walks to door, opens it, greets Rabbi Madoff.]

RABBI	*(Approaching fireplace)* I hope I'm not interrupting.
MICHEL	Not at all. I was just having a drink by the fire.

132

Can I get you one?

RABBI   No thank you. I won't be long.

               [*Sound: They ease into their seats.*]

RABBI   How are you feeling?

MICHEL   I'm not feeling much of anything, actually. *(Beat)* Numb's the word.

RABBI   Have you spoken with Evelyn since our talk?

MICHEL   No. But I've heard from the Canadian Jewish Council. They're not giving me the medal.

RABBI   I'm sorry.

MICHEL   If only Marowitz —

RABBI   You should thank Henry Marowitz.

MICHEL   I will nev —

RABBI   Yes, thank him. For forcing you to confront what you would have left buried. It is too late to save Aaron Farber. You can still save yourself.

MICHEL   I saved myself a long time ago.

RABBI   How so?

MICHEL   What happened to Aaron Farber changed my life.

RABBI   Indeed.

MICHEL   The path I pursued is a matter of public record.

RABBI   Then it is in your best interests to make a public statement.

               [*A lull as the rabbi's words hover between them.*]

RABBI   I have a proposition for you.

             [*A moment's silence as each waits for the other to speak.*]

MICHEL   I'm listening.

RABBI   I would like to give you an opportunity to address my congregation. On Friday night. Tell them what needs to be told. Tell them your story. They will see the picture in the paper. They will draw fast, damning conclusions.

MICHEL   They know who I am.

RABBI   And they think they know who you were. (Beat) Invite Evelyn. Use a public podium to forge a private reconciliation.

MICHEL   *(Pause)* I can't.

RABBI   You must.

MICHEL   You expect me to address a hostile audience.

RABBI   I expect you to find the courage to do what is right.

MICHEL   I am not a coward. Nor am I fool. By tomorrow I will have been tried and convicted in the court of public opinion. There is no point trying to save face.

RABBI   Then at the very least you must save your marriage.

             [*We hear the fire, and can all but see Michel staring into it.*]

Scene Twenty: Synagogue

RABBI   Many of you have grown accustomed to my weekly observations. Too accustomed, some would argue.

[Sound: Gentle laughter by congregation.]

RABBI   Tonight, a departure of sorts. I have invited a guest speaker to address you. To my great delight, he has agreed to speak with you, to share a story he has not shared before. Most of you are familiar with his work, his international reputation in the name of human rights.

[Sound: Murmurs of concern from the crowd.]

RABBI   His sterling reputation has been tarnished. The Berman Medal is no longer his. A tarnished reputation, some will say, is a small price compared to what Aaron Farber had to pay.

[Sound: Loud cries of disapproval.]

RABBI   Let us not speak of retribution or revenge. Let us open our hearts and our minds. Lynn Charney of the Canadian Jewish Council is amongst us tonight. She used a phrase I am going to borrow. When we discussed what the newspapers have labelled *l'affaire Beauchemin* — oh, how they love labels — Lynn looked at a tragic moment in our city's history, a remarkable life that stemmed from it, and spoke of "moral soil." How we all have it. How we're born with it. How it sometimes becomes contaminated. Sometimes, it is reclaimed. Let us not speak of retribution. Let us not speak of revenge. Let us speak of reclaiming soil that is rightfully ours. Let us listen to Michel Beauchemin.

[Sound: A barely restrained chorus of disapproval from the congregation, which fades as Michel

makes his way to the podium. They continue to react throughout Michel's speech at moments considered objectionable.]

MICHEL

(Pause) I would like to talk to you about stones. A handful of stones. I once threw a handful of stones. I threw stones at a man I did not know. *(Beat)* Aaron Farber. *(Beat)* I knew Aaron Farber was Jewish. That was all I needed to know. I believed — No. I was made to...moulded to believe that Aaron Farber was a threat to me. Yes. This 64-year-old man was a threat to me, nineteen years old and tall as a tree. This little man, he was a symbol for everybody who was not like me. He was not born here. He did not speak my language. He ate different food. If he...if his kind didn't leave, there would be nothing left for me. That is what I believed. It is what I wanted to believe. And it made me angry. Who can explain the hate of a young man? I binged on nationalism. Extreme nationalism. You see it everywhere. In Quebec. In Canada. *(Beat)* In Israel. Who can explain the blind passion for a nation, a fierce love that feeds on a hatred for immigrants, newcomers, even those who have shared the same soil for generations but have a different last name, a different colour, a different history. When you are angry and you have a stone in your hand, the stone doesn't stay in your hand for long. What happened to Aaron Farber happened quickly. I know I was there. I know I threw some stones. The rest is a blur. *(Pause)* What happened the next day is very clear. There was a picture of Aaron Farber in the newspaper. The late Aaron Farber. In the picture he is holding his grandson. They are both smiling. The grandson, he looks just like my cousin André. I look once, I look twice. I have to rub my eyes to make sure it's not him. I start to shake. I feel sick. I empty my stomach right there on the street. Sometimes, it happens. A picture, a

moment, a gesture can change your life. A few days later I show the picture to my uncle. André's father. He is more like a brother than an uncle. He agrees Farber's grandson looks just like his boy. He asks me why I'm so pale. I tell him what I had done, the way you tell a brother. He takes a long time before speaking. The longer he takes, the more I shrink. By the time he talks, I am the size of an ant. My uncle, he tells me I must go to Aaron Farber. I must apologize and ask for his forgiveness. It's too late, I say. He is dead. My uncle shakes his head. No. It's never too late. How will I find him, I ask. He tells me to go to every Jewish cemetery until I do. *(Pause)* I found Aaron Farber. It was difficult because, as you know, there was no tombstone. The man at the cemetery, he told me about Jewish custom and told me to come back in a year, when the tombstone would be unveiled. He asked me how I knew Aaron Farber. I said nothing. *(Pause)* I kneeled by his gravesite. I apologized. I told him how much his grandson looked like my cousin André. I asked for his forgiveness. I wept so hard, it was like I was watering the ground in which he was buried. A year later, I returned to the cemetery. Aaron Farber had his tombstone. On top of the tombstone I noticed some stones. I asked a woman nearby about the stones. She explained that when you visited the gravesite, you placed a stone on top of the tombstone to show that the deceased had not been forgotten. So I picked up a stone and placed it on Aaron Farber's tombstone. I left a stone every year after that. Year after year after year. I stopped leaving a stone only after I married for the second time, to a beautiful woman who is here tonight. I don't know why I stopped visiting Aaron Farber's gravesite after I married Evelyn. Perhaps...Perhaps I felt it marked a new beginning. Like the day I saw the picture of Aaron Farber's grandson. I knew Aaron Farber could not forgive me. And so I decided the best way to honour him was to live honourably. I have tried my best to do just that. *(Pause)* This morning, I visited a Jewish cemetery for the first time in many, many years. I walked for a long while. I got lost. I kept walking until I found what I was looking for. I picked up a handful of stones and placed them on the tombstone, one at a time.

END

Emil Sher's dramas, fiction, and essays have been widely anthologized. His stage work includes *Derailed*, written in collaboration with Catherine Hayos and Rena Polley of Toronto's Stiletto Company. It was nominated for four 1995 Dora Mavor Moore Awards, including best production. *Sanctuary* has been produced in Toronto and New York and staged at several one-act festivals. Currently, he is adapting *Mourning Dove* for the screen and stage. Other projects include *Face in the Crowd*, a play for young audiences, and *Sophie, So Far*, a book about his first year as a father.

Mourning Dove
Gold Medal, New York Festivals, 1997

"Achingly relevant ... Rooted in the unfathomable complexities of our times. Whatever views you hold on mercy killing, it would be impossible to listen to *Mourning Dove* and not be moved."
— Christopher Harris, *The Globe and Mail*

"*Mourning Dove* is shockingly good radio — maybe even great radio — because it places you in the father's consciousness. It draws together that infinity of issues and questions circling the case into the most intimate drama of feeling."
— Peter Goddard, *Toronto Star*

Denial is a River
Shortlisted by the Writers Guild of Canada as one of the Top Ten scripts of 1996

"An exceptionally powerful and moving drama ... A tightly written, well-acted play that brings home genuine tragedy with an intensity normally beyond the reach of news coverage."
— Bob Blakey, *Calgary Herald*

Past Imperfect
1998 Gabriel Award

"Powerful stuff from Sher ... *Past Imperfect* is a sensitive, thought-provoking play about prejudice, fear, politics, and redemption"
— Mike Boone, *The Gazette*

"A gripping CBC Radio drama ... It seems a recipe for what easily could have become merely an exaggerated morality play. But the complexity of Beauchemin's character as drawn by Sher ... raises it above that."
— Hal Doran, *Ottawa Citizen*